Erii

# NEVADA HIGHLANDER

New Dawn Press

New Dawn Press
Liberty Hill, TX, USA

**NEVADA HIGHLANDER**

Copyright ©2013 by Erin O'Quinn

Print ISBN: 978-1494472580
Digital ISBN: 978-1-310072390

Cover by Dreams2Media

This is a work of fiction. Names, characters, places and incidents either are the product of the author's imagination or are used fictitiously and any resemblance to actual persons, living or dead, business establishments, events or locales is entirely coincidental.

All rights reserved. No part of this book may be used or reproduced or transmitted in any form or by any means, electronic or mechanical, including photocopying, recording, or by any information storage and retrieval system, without written permission from the copyright owner except in the case of brief quotations embodied in critical articles and reviews.

First New Dawn Press electronic publication: December 2013
First New Dawn Press print publication: December 2013

Published in the United States of America with international distribution.

# DEDICATION

To Alex.
You know who you are, my friend and muse.

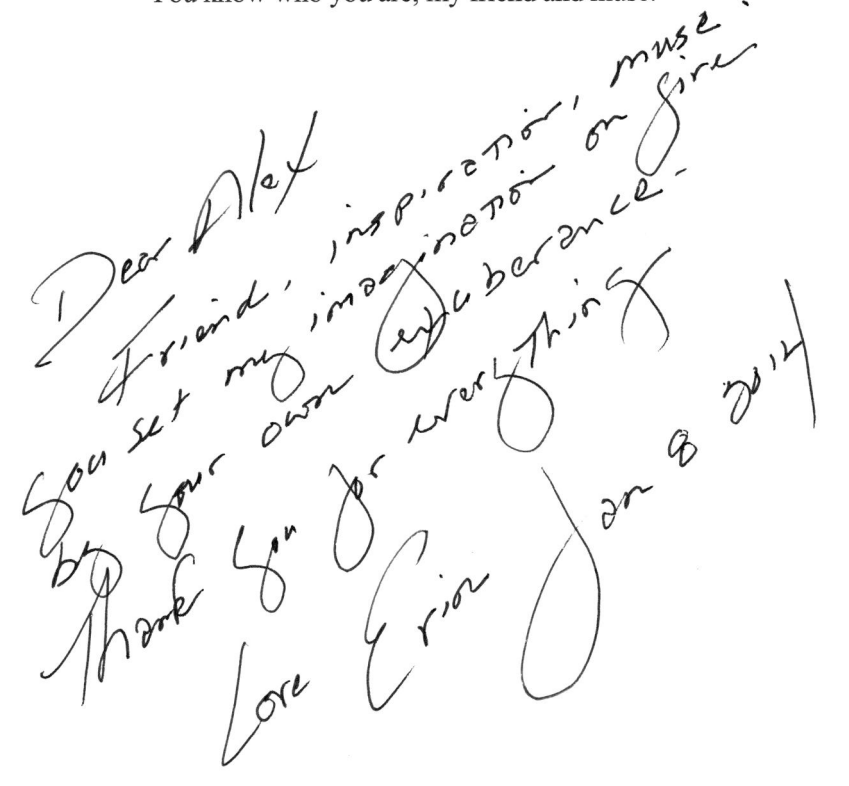

*Dear Alex,
Friend, inspiration, muse!
You set my imagination on fire
by your own exuberance.
Thank you for everything.
Love Erin   Jan 8 2014*

# ACKNOWLEDGMENTS

This book would not have been published without your patient tutelage, Diane. You have given more of yourself than anyone has the right to expect of another. To say "thank you" does not seem nearly enough. To tell the world here is to make the gratitude more tangible, yet still seems somehow inadequate. Thank you, my friend. Maybe the simplest words are the most profound.

To Su and Alex, for your critical eye; and to Rebecca, for your gift of artistry ... I give thanks too.

# FOREWORD TO MY READERS

This novel is set in the "Wilderness Trails" literary universe shared by three novels I have co-authored with Nya Rawlyns, a.k.a. Diane Nelson. Sheriff Cade Wilder and the characters at the Long Trails Ranch were created in our work NIGHT HUNTERS.

The members of Clan Drummond and the honorable Governor of the State of Nevada are emphatically and entirely fictitious. Likewise the air service from the airport called Yelland Field in Eastern Nevada was invented so my characters can arrive and depart in a timely manner; and the particulars about Castle Drummond are figments of my imagination.

# Chapter One
## The Trooper

Alex squirmed in the fancy leather chair whose seat was slick and too hot against his state-issue blue slacks. He longed for the comfort of his Levi's and boots, but that would have to wait. Right now was no doubt the most important interview of his life. He sat up as straight as possible, given the monstrous back of the opulent chair. But then, all the furniture in the Governor's office seemed overdone, out of style. Like something out of the Gilded Age, in an old-time San Francisco brothel.

*Why me?* He'd asked himself a hundred times why he'd been pulled from his lonely vigil of the highways, into the Elko regional office of the Nevada Department of Public Safety. They'd given him a once-over, declared him fit for the next step, and told him to pack and take the next plane for Carson City. To the Governor's office, *por Diós*.

Not a soul would tell him what the hell was going on. The old mushroom theory, he was convinced.

*Keep me in the dark and feed me bullshit. The way bureaucracy works, right?*

Alex knew it was something pretty special. They didn't just pluck state troopers out of their car and put them on a plane for the state capitol, pay for a decent motel. Hell, they didn't even have the extra money to pony up firearms for the troopers. Instead, they made them buy their own. So coughing up money for a cushy vacation in the capitol... It just didn't compute.

Trying to take his mind off the interview scheduled for ten sharp, he tried to look stiffly at attention all the while he let his mind rove back over his short, undistinguished career as a Nevada State Trooper.

He'd been born and raised not too far from his Elko home base, a burg named Ely, the last frontier for those heading south to Vegas or east to Utah along Nevada's notorious lonely highways. He knew, in the old days, Ely was the aftermath of Kennecott Copper's stewardship of the mines that had gone el-foldo, the company taking everything but the gaping maw of a pit and going to Chile, where they could get a better return on the metal, then setting up base later in Utah.

The departure of the mining company had left Ely hardly more than legal gambling joints, a lot of bars, a few schools and churches, and a whole lot of going-nowhere. For fifty years, it had been a town with a past but no future.

His mind skip-jumped over the death of his parents, one after the other, some kind of lung disease, leaving his life like the gaping copper pit—a hole with nothing to fill it. He'd been in seventh grade when his father died; and a year later, his mother fought against the dark until she was gone too.

Somehow, in spite of living in two different foster homes, he'd been a better-than-average student at White Pine High, graduating in the top tenth percentile of his class. He'd been good in language classes, math, even chem. Not quite good enough to win a scholarship to a four-year college. But good enough to know he had a life somewhere outside of Ely, Nevada.

After graduating, he'd worked hard the entire summer, always with the voice of his mother in the back of his skull.

*Alejandro. You will be somebody, sí? Por tu madre.*

He remembered her honey-sweet voice, the determined purse of her lips, her unshakable belief in him. And the ghost of his father walked alongside him still. When summer ended, he took every penny he'd ever saved and hitched a ride to Las Vegas.

He never missed a single class at Clark County Community College. In two years, he had earned an associate's degree. Again, nothing special. One elective class he'd taken, Intro to Criminal Justice, had fired him up. For the first time in his life, he thought he had an idea of what he wanted to do. He wanted to track down bad guys. He wanted to drive a cop car. He wanted to be a different kind of cowboy—maybe one with a motorcycle under his ass and a six shooter on his belt. Someday. Now at twenty-three, he'd been an exemplary trooper for going on four years with nothing more to show for it than sitting in this high-ceilinged room, wondering what the hell was happening to him.

Instead of a bike under his butt, he was sitting with crappy leather eating into his shorts and no firearm at all. Those were not allowed here.

He could daydream about his ass being eaten by something else ... except he'd be lucky to find a real lover. It hadn't happened yet, outside of shitty one-night-stands, and it wasn't likely to happen soon. He naturally shied away from those casual encounters. Plus who the hell would shack up with a state trooper, gone four days out of every week, coming home cranky and exhausted? And yet the image of a hungry mouth and knowing hands on his squirming ass began to shut out the dreariness of sitting here, waiting...

"Mr. Dominguez?"

He snapped out of his trance and jerked his head to the source of the polite voice. "The Governor will see you now."

A few minutes later he was ensconced in another goddamn leather chair, except a lot more comfortable. And the man sitting across from him in the sumptuous room was Governor Escamillo Suarez of the great State of Nevada.

Suarez was not the only non-Anglo governor this state ever had. Alex had heard folks talk about Laxalt, the one whose heritage was Basque, the people whose mysterious language and traditions made them an important symbol of Nevada's diversity. So having a man of Mexican descent run the state was pretty cool. Better than cool, he thought. In this day of cutthroat political divisions, with Suarez being a Republican, it was downright miraculous.

After shaking hands, he and the governor had chatted lightly about his trip, the blasted cold front that had moved across the state, a little about his growing up in Ely. And then the bomb dropped.

"Mr. Dominguez ... mind if I call you Alex?" To his shake of the head, Suarez continued, "I find myself in a kind of, er, uh, a diplomatic stew." He grinned. "I like a good old-fashioned beef stew. The diplomatic kind sticks in my craw a little, I have to admit."

The governor had brown-black eyes with generous smile crinkles at the corners and a ready grin. As if drawing Alex into his confidence, he leaned toward him with his fingers steepled on the marble desktop and lowered his voice like a co-conspirator.

"In a word, I've been asked by a high-ranking man in Scotland to provide protection for one of his own. A Scottish lord of some kind, hell, I'm not sure. But he's the nephew of some big shot in the Parliament there. And someone in Washington has called to remind me about it. So I'm in a kind of a squeeze I can't rightly wriggle out of."

"Um, why here, sir? Why would some Scottish lord want to come here?"

"Not here, not Carson City, Alex. The man has decided he wants to be a big game hunter. Wants to shoot up elk and deer and whatnot. He—or probably his people—have lit on a place not too far from your home town. In the Snake Valley, the..." He paused to extract a piece of paper from a file folder. "The Long Trails Ranch, big game hunts for a big price. Ever heard of them?"

"No, sir. But I think Snake Valley would be a good place to center a big game hunt type of ranch. Close to Mt. Moriah, lots of elk and mule deer, even bighorn sheep. Now, close to winter is a great time to hunt. Even in the spring..." He stopped talking. No sense babbling when this man had more to tell him.

"Keep talking, Alex."

"It's nothing, sir. I have ... ah, my father used to take me hunting out there. I know the land pretty well. I know it's pretty much a wilderness. Not an easy way to bag a deer."

Suarez was listening closely. "This is great, just great. Your knowledge is partly why I chose you."

"Chose me, sir?"

"Alex, I've looked at your school records." He paused and picked up another few pieces of paper and glanced at them. "You're smart. Got an A in Criminal Justice, A's in most of your other work. I see you've had classes in all kinds of martial arts. You're apparently a fine shooter. I see at a glance, you keep yourself fit. Your record with the DPS is sterling."

He set the papers aside and leaned in again. "Plus, you're a native son, so to speak. Grew up right around those parts, know the people, know how to talk the talk.

"I want you to be the escort of this pooh-bah. You can tell him and the others you have an extended vacation, you've always wanted to shoot a deer, *blah blah blah*. But without getting this Scotsman's kilt in a knot, you're there to protect him. Keep him from shooting his own damn toe off, or falling down the mountain. I also get the hint that he may be a bit of a, erm, partier. Keep him from calling undue attention to himself. Think you can do that?"

Alex was caught off guard. He would love to show his martial expertise, his shooting ability, his way of blending in with almost anybody. But to be a goddamned babysitter? Or a morals cop? Pretend to be a friend when he wasn't? Something about the assignment hit him below the belt, gave him a stomach ache from the balls up. It would mean living a lie. Not his style. He'd never aspired to be an undercover cop.

He tried to look someplace other than Suarez' keen gaze, but it was no use. "Sir. I ... feel not worthy of this assignment. There are so many others..." It wasn't a matter of being worthy, but b.s. by any other name was always expedient. The fact that it came out stilted, as though his tongue wasn't quite wrapping around the concept, simply told the governor he could use a remedial course in suck-up.

"Bullshit!" The governor, incredibly, was smiling. "I've chosen you. You, Dominguez. Are you telling me I'm full of crap?"

Alex knew he was cornered, by a man who'd probably played political games most of his life. "No, no, not at all. Sir."

"Then I'll consider it a personal favor if you will accept this assignment. I've seen five other guys. You are my choice. Okay?"

Put that way, Alex knew he was being offered something more than an ass-wipe job. Five other applicants... If he could show this man he was worthy... Maybe his future would hold more than a four-on-three-off shift on the endless lonesome road his life had become.

"Okay. I accept."

"My secretary George Braxton will fill you in on the details."

He stood, and Alex did too. Instead of leaning across the desk, Suarez stepped from behind the marble behemoth and walked up to him, extending his hand.

"I know I chose well. I'll read your report in a week or so, when it's over. Satisfactorily over, right?"

Alex managed a brief smile at the smallish fellow with the sparkling eyes.

"Right. Sir."


Alex had plenty of time on the plane trip to Yelland Field outside of Ely to think about what had happened.

The governor had shanghaied him with his charm and his seeming faith that Alex was the go-to guy for a delicate job. He still felt like the man had cornered him, made it impossible for him to back out and keep face. To turn down the assignment, as Suarez had hinted, was to spit in the eye of the big man himself.

Alex had a sneaking hunch his own Hispanic surname had helped narrow the search a little. And he had felt a certain ... lingering in the governor's handshake that told him Suarez liked eye candy. But at least he hadn't been obvious about it.

He shifted a little in the too-small seat and reflected on his own appearance. He was a regular at Bo's Work Out Gym whenever he came into Elko, to his small apartment, on his days off. He kept himself at a trim one-ninety, had shoulders that a few men and women had told him went into forever. No one could fault his long legs and tight ass either.

A few women had told him, with adoration on their faces, that he looked "just like Juanes." Meaning the Colombian singer, twice his age, who actually did have fuck-me eyes and shimmering dark hair. Why didn't a sexy man ever tell him the same thing? *Because most men look at crotches and asses, that's why.*

So why couldn't he score a halfway decent roll in the sack?

After debating with himself for years, after chewing his inner cheeks raw over it on the long drives, Alex had finally decided maybe it wasn't his looks. It could be his attitude.

He couldn't stand phonies, first off. Anyone with a smile too wide, a certain way of handing out blandishments, of spreading the free drinks and dishing out the lingering arm squeezes—anyone who approached him that way might as well try somebody else. He wanted to talk about hunting, sports, weapons and ammo. Or not talk at all. He wanted a man to appeal to his serious side. He longed for subtlety.

There was one other tiny factor at play. Alex admitted he was a naturally reserved man. He'd grown up an only child, had never learned the interpersonal skills to do more than fold into a corner even at family gatherings. And then four years of going from one foster home to another, where he longed for any kind of privacy... He was always inclined to sit back and listen and observe. No wonder his social life hung in the balance between zilch and zero.

He'd decided to hang up the idea of having a real lover. He'd rather wait until kingdom come than settle for the guys at the gym, the ones at the bars he tried, the few on the force who'd actually approached him. He'd gotten to be a one-minute marvel at jacking off, not even thinking about it, just blowing off the pent-up needs of a healthy young guy.

He stared out the window as his body felt the unmistakable slowing of the engines, the plane's gliding descent. Below, gray clouds covered the ground. He was seeing the tail-end of one helluva storm that had gripped Eastern Nevada for two days in an early embrace. Usually the heavy white stuff didn't arrive until November. But now, leaning into late October, he knew the Wheeler and Snake ranges wore a new coat rapidly becoming ice. He knew also the mule deer and elk would be making their sure way down Mt. Moriah, looking for winter browse under the fresh snow.

A perfect time for a hunt. He was actually looking forward to that part of his assignment. Before his father had died, back when he was in grade school, Ramón Dominguez had faithfully taken his only son to the Moriah area every year. Taught him how to handle game rifles, how to use night scopes, the right way to use the landscape itself as a wilderness home. That expertise was part of his Colombian heritage, a kind of survival instinct his *compadres* and his family carried always. After his parents died he'd been forced to use those survival skills at an early age.

Now, going back, it was almost as though his father was standing up there among the sentinel bristlecones, waiting to rejoin him. He'd deliberately not returned to Moriah. *Maybe it's time.*

He thought again about his assignment, about the unnamed stuffed shirt he was supposed to shield without shielding. No doubt spoiled by a life of indolence and wealth. Maybe even trained to hunt ... whatever they hunted in Scotland. Foxes? Birds? He wished he'd had the time to do some internet browsing before he got hustled onto the Air Force plane bringing him here.

How would this Scottish *cabrón* like the temps here in Nevada? Maybe after one day he'd button up his kilt and make for Southern California, like any reasonable tourist. Or New Mexico. Yeah, give the guy a day to shiver his butt off and decide to leave for warmer climes.

Someone had arranged for a man from the local sheriff's office to meet and greet him, set him up for a talk with the ranch owner. Because you don't have some doofus guy suddenly show up on a big game hunt and demand a license and a place in the food line. Somebody had to pay some big bucks for the possibility of big bucks. The governor's secretary had already taken care of that. All he had to do was make nice with the sheriff and the bigwig putting on the hunt. He thought he was up to it.

The man who met him stood rock-still with a strange look on his face. Like he was reading his character from a distance and deciding whether to turn on his heel and leave. "Alex Dominguez?"

"The same."

The man in front of him looked directly into his eyes. Not too many people stood six-foot-two, so Alex felt somehow he was meeting an equal ... except way up the food chain from his lowly trooper status.

They shook briefly. "Cade Wilder. County Sheriff. Ah, I'm to take you to meet the man who runs the hunts. It's just noon. Let's grab a cuppa coffee in the lounge before we hit the road."

Settling down at a back table, Alex looked closely at his companion. The sheriff was a man maybe five or so years older than himself. His eyes were the color of ... mink maybe, a deep rich brown. His hair had a habit of falling over his forehead, and the sheriff himself kept brushing it back with one thumb. A nice looking man who seemed to be all business, in spite of the little-boy gesture with his thumb. The all-business part pleased Alex. His kind of law enforcement officer.

Wilder came right to the point. "You're gonna have one helluva time convincing Long to let this whole scenario play out, at least the secretive part. He's been bitten once by just this kind of crap. An undercover marshal babysitting a Mafia figure. Ended in a manhunt that put a lot of folks in danger, and not just him. He makes no bones about never playing that game, ever again."

Alex drew in a long breath. "Look. I'm undercover only to the Kilt. Far as I'm concerned, Long and his people can be in on the game. Just so they don't give away my role. So the Kilt won't think I'm babysitting him."

"When in fact that's just what you're doing."

"You know the deal, huh?"

"Been there, done that."

"I know nothing about the man. I just know that someone in Scotland called someone in Washington, who called the governor."

"Who then called you."

"Um, in a way. What I mean is, Sheriff, the Scottish guy's no doubt a tenderfoot, needs someone to keep a close eye on his ass. Better me than this fellow Long or his own men. I'm polite, mostly. I keep to myself. I know how to shoot. I can get along with my fellow man when necessary."

He saw Wilder grin a little and returned it. "Honest. Take me to him, and I think I can convince him."

"I promise you, it'll be harder to convince Steve Long than to take care of some tourist in a kilt. A lot harder."

"Take me there, Sheriff. I can only try."

Before they walked outside, both men zipped their winter jackets to the chin and leaned into the wind, heading for the long, dry valley folks called the Snake.

NEVADA HIGHLANDER

# Chapter Two
## The Laird

Rory Drummond flicked the edge of his dress jacket where it crossed his midriff, erasing a tiny wrinkle. His stomach was muscular, flat and athletic, and the crinkling looked somehow out of place. Not bothering to hide his thighs under the kilt, he sat open-kneed in the Moroccan leather chair Robert Drummond gestured to.

*Foogin leather.*

The chair seat rubbed his balls, and not kindly. He adjusted his ass a little, leaning forward to greet his uncle.

Robert poured a drink and waved the crystal decanter his way. "Whisky?"

"Of course."

His uncle walked across the deep-pile oriental rug to where he sat and extended the glass. Not bothering to sip it, Rory let the amber liquid fire his throat, then his gut in one long swallow before raising his glass with a grin of appreciation.

"Irish?"

"American. Wild Turkey."

Rory almost did a spit-take. "Wild *what*?"

Robert swept back the long tail of his afternoon jacket and sat across from him on a slightly more comfortable-looking divan. "I thought ... since you're determined to be a frontiersman ... you need to drink their whisky. I could even arrange a saloon girl for the afternoon, if you want to fuck one of their women." He winked, a subtle gesture only Rory would have seen, and lifted his own glass.

Rory made a face but said nothing. His uncle was trying to piss him off, but he wasn't taking the bait. He felt too good about his upcoming adventure.

"Laugh if you will, Robbie me lad. I have an itch. And I will scratch it."

Robert leaned forward a bit, his handsome face betraying nothing of his real thoughts. That's why the man was a famed politician, Rory knew. *Give away nothing to your opponent. Ever.* And at this indolent moment, two o'clock of an afternoon in a posh office of the Scottish Parliament Building, he was not a nephew but an adversary. He hadn't exactly been summoned here, but he'd gotten the clear hint that Robert wanted to bid him *bon voyage* before his flight out of Edinburgh Airport.

"Scratch away, Rory. Just don't show the, ah, wart on your ass while you're doing it." He hid his face in the gleaming facets of the cut-glass goblet as he drank, leaving Rory to fume inside.

Rory Drummond, laird of Drummond Castle in Arbroath, Scotland, drank again to hide his suddenly sour mood. Why couldn't Robert stay out of his bloody business?

He tossed down the remaining splash of remarkably good whiskey and stood, this time adjusting the waistcoat of his dress kilt, before striding to the liquor cabinet and pouring his own drink. Twice as many fingers tall as Robert had poured.

"And what wart is that, Uncle Robbie?"

"Just be careful. I have an election coming up in precisely three months. You know that. The family name is centuries old, bathed in glory. I wish to keep it that way."

Rory grinned and sat back, legs again splayed, knowing he was revealing a huge amount of manhood. On a bloke his size, that hood was a force to reckon with.

*Screw Robert. Down deep, the man's a prude. Let him see how a real Scot sits in a goddamn uncomfortable chair.*

He drank again, this time to calm his annoyance. "I am always discreet, Rob. You know that."

The slightest crease skidded across the space above the Parliamentarian's eyebrows. "Rory. If you are always discreet, why is it I know about Ian? And—who was it before that—ah, yes, Jack?"

Determined not to rise to the bait, Rory laid his head back and grinned. His nosy uncle obviously was ill-informed. There had been at least three since Ian and Jack. "Because you set your spies on me, I'm supposed to tremble and quail and beg forgiveness? I'm only sorry that neither of those men could satisfy a foogin billy goat."

Robert set his drink on an ornate parquet side table, then leaned toward him even more. A sign of his earnestness, Rory thought.

"Rory Drummond. You are family. And as such, I feel a certain, ah, affection for you. Always have. But you must respect my own life, my ambitions. I want you to conduct yourself with utmost discretion while you ... do whatever safari hunters do. Shoot the moose, bag the turkey, win the trophy. But remember your family. Remember your own reputation must be impeccable. Yes?"

Rory sat up straight and took another generous swallow. "I understand better than you can possibly know, Robbie Drummond. I am a castle laird, a respected man. My private life is just that. Utterly private. Until someone sets a spyglass on my bloody bedroom window. Which will stop immediately, I am sure. Because I would hate to embarrass ... anyone at all."

He shot Robert his danger eye, the glare he knew could set grown men to crying. He might be a gay man, but he was a large and strong and perilous gay man. Let not Robert be deceived just because they were blood relatives.

"Of course, dear Rory. Let the subject be considered dead and buried. What do you think about this sudden lurch to the right of the Labour Party? I think I can use..."

Rory stopped listening and started counting the minutes until he left the airport. Forty-eight hours and he'd be free to do whatever he goddamn wanted to do. Without Robert's microscope. He settled back and drank the whisky he thought could easily become his favorite, thinking about the ramifications of both *wild* and *turkey*.

Rory considered himself a wild man, but not in the sense his uncle would ever understand. At almost six and a half feet, he was a veritable giant among normal people, one to draw the eye, especially since he was also endowed with russet-red hair, a trim beard, and piercing green eyes which could pin an opponent from twenty feet. Rory Drummond knew he was different.

He'd studied several branches of the martial arts from the time he was a school boy, with tutors brought into the castle by his father. Often his own sire had taught him the finer points of many a hidden art. Even if he'd never learned to thrust and parry, to grapple with an opponent, to kick-box or any of the other techniques he'd mastered ... even if he were a quiet, unassuming man, he'd be frightening to most people. He knew that. He accepted it. Actually, he played it down. Why bother to show off, when he could handle any situation which might present itself?

He was wild also in his choice of bed-mates. All beguiling, and all male. What Robert did not know was that his nephew Rory was not a slut, as Americans on TV called a woman who spread her legs at will. Or a man, for that matter. His choices were, he thought, highly discriminating—even if they had never lasted more than a few weeks. Usually one disappointing night. What Robert disapproved of was not his sex life, but the sex of his partners.

As far as being a turkey ... he understood that term all too well. The turkey had been Benjamin Franklin's choice for the symbol of America. He knew there were small pockets in Scotland where wild turkeys had been introduced, although he'd never hunted them. They were a large beast, an outsized bird just like he was. The juveniles, called jakes, had a short red beard, not unlike his own. He also knew Franklin thought of the birds as courageous, a fitting symbol of a young country rebelling against the yoke of oppression. Yes, the turkey was a fine symbol. And a damned good bourbon whisky. Chalk one up to Robert.

When his uncle stood, so did Rory, glad to leave this close atmosphere of innuendo. He thought Robert wielded the stiletto of deadly politics all too well. And he himself was rather adept with handling the deadlier undercurrent of promise and deceit. He thought he knew much more about his uncle than his uncle knew about him.

Craving the outside air, he gladly followed Robert through the elaborate door. He wanted to be out in his beloved Cairngorm Mountains, or on a distant peak in Nevada, far from those who would train their eye on his every move.

Any other time, Rory would have lingered in the unique building housing the distinguished Scottish Parliament. Not quite ten years old, to him it was a triumph of granite and gneiss, traditional stone of his country, combined with delicate sweeps of curved glass; and subtle patterns of leaves, twigs and grass. Even if the public at large was ready to blow its collective gasket over the architecture and its perceived excesses, to Rory it was a place to contemplate the relation between man and nature, between the mighty and the meek.

He said as much to Robert as they descended the processional staircase leading to the famous Garden Room. "Mighty and meek, eh? Who are the mighty, nephew? Are you suggesting we humble elected officers somehow look down on our electorate?"

"I'm suggesting, Unc, this building should make all who walk and work here pause and think about what their calling really is."

"Ever the philosopher, Rory lad. You are too much a son of the soil, I think." He stopped as they were about to exit the building and gestured to the renowned ceiling, a study in leaf-shaped glass and steel and oak.

"Look up, always. And there find your center. I must leave you. I trust you've found your hotel accommodations adequate? And you have everything necessary to flee our proud country?"

Rory shook Robert's proffered hand and left him, happy to breathe the brisk air of an Edinburgh late afternoon, just bordering on seven degrees Celsius. "Forty-five, lad. Forget not, you must shiver in Fahrenheit for two weeks."

Outside, Rory paused to admire the sweeping stands of native grass and wildflowers the architect had made sure to integrate with the Parliament grounds. He thought the man, a Catalán named Miralles, was a genius. Rory had loved everything Hispanic most of his life, and this building seemed to him the tangible expression of everything he admired.

*Only a foreigner could have seen our nature and revealed it to us here, in this genius of a building ... on these rugged grounds. A mirror set on these cliffs so we can see ourselves better. Man of Hispania, meet the man of Scotia. We are brothers, you and I.*

From a distance he saw his steward Alan Cameron sitting at the appointed bench, calmly feeding a cluster of pigeons. Rory slowed a little, wanting to enjoy these last few minutes of total aloneness. He let the wind whip the edges of his heavy walking kilt, hardly feeling the cold, and contemplated the slate-blue sky.

Robert was right in one regard. He needed to look up every so often and by doing that, ironically, ground himself.

He asked himself for the millionth time why he was so unsatisfied with his life, one of wealth and possessions. Along with his father Kenneth, he owned a small castle—rustic, warm, beautiful in its simplicity. He had a stable of thoroughbreds, a sailboat, game rooms and work out areas. He had access to any place in Scotland that beckoned.

Then why was he plagued with unrest? Why did he want to sit on a mountain in the unknown state of Nevada, United States of America? Why couldn't he accept his life, live it to the fullest, right here in his homeland?

He wished he could ask the architect, "Why go to Scotland? Why erect a monument to a foreign land, when you could bring joy to your own people of Spain?" But Miralles was dead. No revelation from that end. So the answer to his question must come from inside himself.

So far, in twenty-eight years, he'd not been able to answer that simple question. Why did he always need to run? What was chasing his ass?

*Maybe I'm chasing something, and not the other way around.*

That sudden thought made him grin and look down from the graying sky, just as Alan looked across the plaza at him. Both of them raised an arm in greeting, and Rory hunched his shoulders into the wind as he strode to join his castle steward and right-hand man.

In Scotland this time of year, the sun set around four o'clock. Not much opportunity to do more than go back to the hotel, maybe do some last-minute shopping before a late-ish dinner. They were walking in a vaguely western direction, toward the nest of hotels and shops erected during the construction of the Parliament building a decade ago.

"What think you, Alan? Do you feel like indulging my latest fancy?"

The man who walked next to him in a sober brown wool suit raised his blond head to meet his gaze and grinned. "Always a challenge, sir."

Rory felt like kissing the man on each ruddy cheek. Here was a virtual servant, one who was ready to respond to his every whim, yet impeccably educated and articulate. A steward who was much more. A confidant, a private secretary, one he trusted with every aspect of his business affairs ... and personal affairs too. Alan was a family man. He and his wife and one child lived on the castle grounds. And yet he unfailingly turned his head when Rory brought home his latest conquest. And he never shied from handing the unfortunate bloke his coat and hat the next morning.

"I want a ... a pair of American Levi's. Denim trousers. They look damn sexy on a man. And a western shirt. Cowboy boots too, I think."

He'd done his homework. He knew the temperatures they'd encounter meant heavy wool clothing, layers of underwear, wool stockings, sensible hiking boots. Hell, he already owned that kind of clothing, already packed and waiting in his luggage. What he wanted was something to wake up the sleeping side of him. The wild turkey. He couldn't help grinning and clapping Alan on the back.

"I will be a Nevada highlander, Alan me lad. A celtic cowboy. When I leave, they'll tell stories about me for years to come."

"Um, we can always hope not, sir."

Both of them laughed, then ducked their heads again as they walked into the blustery wind.

The next two days were an unremarkable sequence of shopping, eating, and pacing his hotel room. Nothing would satisfy his itch to leave this place of his birth. Not that he didn't love bonnie Scotland. His uncle had put his finger on it: he was truly a son of the soil. Born and raised in Angus, the cradle of Scotland ... one who escaped to the Cairngorms or to the shore at every opportunity ... a man who'd graduated *summa cum laude* from Edinburgh University, studying the archaeology of Scotland. He'd climbed damn near every peak in the country, examined thousands of cairns, gone deerstalking and pheasant shooting. He'd ridden and walked thousands of square miles in his short life, all of it a joy.

No, his need to leave had much more to do with his feeling of being a specimen in a shadow box. There was nothing he did, nowhere he went, no man he bedded, without the knowledge that he was being watched by his venerable uncle Robert. And all to protect the man's political ambitions.

He loved his flawed relative. But by God, he'd never found a way to escape his gimlet eye. Robert was terrified that Rory would cause a scandal, do something to explode his rising star as maybe the next PM of Scotland. A nephew who loved his men and his whisky was a threat to the future of Robert Drummond. That same gay nephew going to the United States was slightly less frightening to him, Rory suspected. Robert had long arms. But not that long.

In two days, he'd slept about four hours total. And yet when Alan finally poured him onto the plane, Rory was happy as he'd been in years.

"I know the castle is in good hands, lad. I'll not worry one minute about my affairs here. Of course my father will step in as vice-laird, so you may enjoy some needed rest. And I want you to write yourself a check right now for five hundred pounds, for the extra effort these past few weeks. Quick, while I'm sober enough to sign it."

Alan had shooed him all the way to the boarding gate, and they'd embraced quickly—a gentleman and his steward, a man and his friend. He stood in the line dressed in his authentic Nevada costume: Levi's, a handsome fringed shirt, a pair of alligator-skin boots. Too bad none of the stores could ferret out a cowboy hat. No doubt the nearby village would accommodate him when he got there. He referred to the handy guide that Alan had drawn up for him. "Ely. As in Britain's cathedral city."

And then he'd slept almost the entire trip, awake only long enough to stumble to the privy or to eat. He was vaguely aware of changing planes in Houston, Texas to get to a tiny air strip somewhere near that same Ely; and when he felt the plane's final descent, he felt his stomach begin to flip and his hands start to shake.

*I'm here. By God, I'm free.*

# Chapter Three
## Buddies

The Long Trails Ranch was not extensive. Alex understood Steve Long's business was not cattle or horses, but big game expeditions. Alex thought the entire spread might be somewhere short of two hundred acres tucked into Snake Valley by a few quadrants of neat cedar-and-wire fencing. He saw a lone drover in the distance, riding a horse behind maybe thirty head of slow-poke cattle.

Above the ranch, dominating his own imagination, rose the Snake Range and the welcoming profile of Mt. Moriah. He felt a knot in his throat, tried to swallow, realized he was feeling a pang of homesickness. The range wore a mantle of snow, one he knew would melt in a few days with any kind of warm front moving from Salt Lake or Santa Fe across the mountains. By the same token, a blast of air from Canada could change that mantle to a heavy blanket in a matter of hours.

He and Sheriff Wilder drove the black-and-white up the wide, curving path to the front of a sprawling ranch house. He had little time to see more than a barn and a few other livestock outbuildings. As they'd driven up, he'd seen behind the house a grove of mesquite and scrub pine sheltering some small cabins.

"I'm gonna introduce you to Steve Long, then visit my gelding."

To Alex's raised brows, the sheriff smiled. "I board my horse Whiskers here. Long story, ah, so to speak. Good home."

Alex stood on a nicely constructed porch of cedar and pine, its fragrance again taking him back more than a decade, to his days out in that valley, those mountains, with his father. Since then, he hadn't returned, even for a brief visit. Some ghost from his past, maybe? As much as he loved his Moriah, he naturally shied from reliving old memories. He reckoned he was better off keeping his eyes to the future.

The sheriff rapped twice on the door, and it opened almost instantly. He had a fleeting impression of two large men locked in more than friendship as they clasped hands, spoke in brief murmurs to each other, then stood apart.

"Steve, this here is Alex Dominguez. Wants to join the hunt. I'll let you fellows talk while I visit my friend Whiskers, okay?" Without so much as asking for a cup of hot coffee, Wilder turned and walked down the porch stairs, toward the barn.

That left him alone with a very tall man with dark hair and a short, dark beard ... one he sensed was his instant adversary. They were still standing on the porch. The one who blocked his entrance to the house had a good two inches on him, and his blue-chipped eyes seem to slice through his skin and bone. He did not extend his hand.

"May as well come on in, Mr. Dominguez."

He followed Long down a hallway hung with Indian blankets and native paraphernalia, then into a tiny office. Long entered first and sat not behind but next to a battered desk, in a leather chair which might have been new when settlers crossed the plains. He sank into the folds and creases, unfolded his endless legs and gestured with one hand.

"Close that door, wouldya. Have a seat."

The only other place to sit in the room, thank God, was not leather. It was a sturdy wooden captain's style chair with rounded armrests, only slightly newer than the grungy old seat his host was ensconced in.

"Talk to me, Mr. Dominguez. I've heard from the governor's office, of course. I told them this whole idea was mine to approve or disapprove. This is my ranch, my operation, my hunt. Tell me why I should go along with what I consider a hare-brained scheme. Why I should allow a non-hunter to stalk a non-deer."

Long glared at him with flat eyes that could pick apart a combination lock. Then he leaned back, allowed one hand to toy with his clipped beard, and shut his eyes, almost as though he wasn't listening at all.

Alex hadn't counted on this implacable attitude. He'd been hoping to appeal to an unknown rancher's need for money, first of all, finding an instantly-paid addition to his hunt. He thought the State had probably forked over a bundle for Alex's sudden intrusion. He was also hoping he might win a stranger with his own plight, "Hey, I'm just a pawn of the governor, I mean you no harm" kind of line. He realized beyond a doubt that Steve Long neither needed him nor wanted him. Period. So he simply told the truth.

He drew in a deep breath and began to speak as Alex, not as State Trooper Alex Dominguez. "Mr. Long. This assignment feels like someone stuck a jackknife in my gut. I'm the kind of guy who finds his peace out on the open highway, or on a mountain trail. Not with a bunch of other people. Not playing some kind of game. And it numbs my nuts to think I might come off as someone I'm not."

Steve Long suddenly sat up straight in the chair and targeted him with the steel of his voice. "I don't want to know who you're not, I want to know who you are."

"I ... I'm an Ely boy. Born and raised. Went to White Pine High. Fair to middling grades. Then got an Associate's Degree from the community college in 'Vegas. Did okay there too. Been a State Trooper going on four years. Good record." He sat forward in the stiff chair, finding a kind of comfort there, and put his elbows on his knees. "That tells you what? Not much. Except ... I'm kind of a quiet guy, serious about my work, not a glad-hander. Don't suppose I'll ever make the grade as an undercover operative. Because the truth goes down a lot easier than a lie."

Steve Long opened his eyes. "You said you were comfortable on a mountain trail. Tell me about that."

"Well, sir, my father and me ... we used to damn near live up there on Mt. Moriah, when I didn't have to be in school. Deer hunting, hiking, fishing. That was before, uh..."

Now the man actually unwound himself from his place of solace and stood, regarding him with a cock of his head. "Mt. Moriah? When was this?"

"Back when I was in grade school. Late nineties, early 2K."

"And your father's name?"

"Ramón."

"By God, I knew your father. I even knew you, in a way. Good-looking kid with a face full of very dark eyes. Shy. Protective of your old man." He grinned. "I knew Ray pretty damn well, back when I was a game warden. At least to share a meal with, sit around a fire with, tell tall tales with. Haven't seen him for ... it has to be more than ten years."

"He's dead. Him and my mom both. Lung disease. Took them quick. Part of the reason I haven't come back here, not wanting to poke the ashes of old campfires."

Steve sat again, this time leaning toward him, imitating his own posture, forearms on knees. His eyes had taken on a different look altogether, as though eyes held the secret to a man's mind. His seemed to say, *I understand.*

"Alex. Listen to me. Your father was a good man. One of the best. I'm sorry he's gone. But maybe being here again will be—oh, I don't know, a blessing. A way of sorting out the past, making it jibe with the present."

The words sank into his flesh, almost a warm handshake welcoming him, and goddamn if he didn't feel a tightness in his throat he used to feel before he cried. Something he hadn't done in a very long time. And he remembered this man, now that the mask of cold eyes had disappeared. That long-ago man had no beard, but a head of long hair that stood up almost straight when he ran his hands through it. That man had come around three or four times, always in some kind of official shirt, always polite, often laughing. One his father liked. It all came rushing back.

When he looked at the man across from him, he knew there was a sheen on his own eyes, but he didn't dare wipe the back of his hand across them like a kid.

"So I guess now you know everything. I agreed to this because the governor told me he chose me personally. Liked something about me. Refusing him was like, almost like diminishing him in a way. Telling him he was wrong. So here I am."

"Okay, Alex. I think we can work this out. Have you thought about how you can be a straight shooter, and still be someone you're not?"

Those words hurt, a lot. Steve Long had put his finger on exactly why he still felt like a betrayer.

"I have, sir. I thought of something maybe you already do on your hunts, with your guests. Not sure it would work..."

"Tell me, damn it."

"I thought maybe you could set up a buddy system. Where two people are set up as buddies, having each other's back. They could bunk together, share a tent, even hunt in buddy groups, as long as at least one of them can half-ass handle a rifle. So me and my Scotsman would be buddies. And I pray to God he doesn't snore too loud, and hope he can live with my stinky feet."

"Ha! By God, Alex, I never even thought of that. One hell of an idea. That would take a lot of pressure off my own boys. They have enough trouble making sure none of the fledgling hunters break a leg or shoot themselves. Or each other. Fuck, it just might work."

"That way, I don't have to live a lie. I'll be watching him. And he'll be watching me. Like friends. That I can live with. I can probably even learn to enjoy it."

"Okay. I'm convinced. Come on with me to the dining room for a cup of coffee, and I'll haul Cade outta the barn to join us. And I'll show you your new cabin in the woods."

Alex turned to open the door, and Steve Long patted him on the shoulder. "Call me Steve. And welcome." He held out his hand, and when they shook it felt like he was grasping a branch of timber, strong and sure, a promise of friendship.

"Thank you, Steve. I feel almost like a new man already."


Alex took stock of his temporary shelter, the small cabin he and his unknown buddy were to share for the next day or so, until all the would-be hunters gathered. The word "cabin" didn't begin to hint at the smallness. It was about ten by fifteen feet, with one end screened by a cheap shower curtain to give some privacy to whoever needed to take a crap or a very fast, cold shower.

There were two narrow cots in the little shelter, far enough apart for a man to walk between, not much wider. A metal contraption with empty hangers stood on one wall opposite the vinyl sheet. There were no curtains at all on the lone window which looked out over a cluster of mesquite and white pines.

One transformer-operated space heater stood near the end Steve had euphemistically called the "bathroom." Enough to take the chill off the room, but just barely. Two straight-backed wooden chairs completed the suite.

Alex shrugged mentally. His own cramped apartment was only a few notches above this one. He'd get by. He grinned, thinking of the Scottish lord who would no doubt be looking for his valet, bun warmer, and jacuzzi.

When he'd left Elko, they'd told him to pack warm clothes and hiking boots. Period. No other clue as to what his future held. Again, the image of a blustery highlander rose before his eyes, dressed in a dainty skirt and a cap topped with a pom-pom. That was his idea of highlander wear, untouched by internet images or any scholarship at all. He simply hadn't had the time to look up Scotland before he'd landed right here in this room. He thought he'd learn by the more sure method—rubbing shoulders with a real Scotsman.

*Hell, small as this place is, we'll be rubbing more than elbows.* He shook his head, wondering how he could erect a privacy screen between the two cots without looking like a total dick. He decided that wouldn't be possible. *Better buy some kind of pajamas.*

It was going on two o'clock, and Steve had told him his buddy was due to arrive at the air field around four. As they sat nursing coffee mugs in Steve's big dining room, he'd mentioned the man was coming in early, a day ahead of the others, and he'd admitted the notion was enough to put his mood a little south of foul.

"But now he has a buddy, right, Alex?" He grinned and dug in a Levi's pocket, hauling out two keys on a ring. "Why don't you pick him up for me? That way I don't have to send one of my own men. I'm sure he went through Customs in Houston. But there'll still be a lot of rigamarole getting him here." He tossed the keys, which Alex caught with one hand.

"Chevy sports van, the one with the Long Trails sign on the door. Hell, you can take him to dinner and a dance, for all I care. Come back when you're ready. If you stay late, breakfast is served at six. You ain't here, we eat anyway."

He'd had the suspicion as he left that Steve and Cade were relieved to be alone. Just a hunch. But he had some small ability to read men, and he knew those two intense men shared something deeper than casual friendship. *Good on 'em.* He wished he was lucky enough to have a partner half as great as either of those guys. Or any partner at all.

He decided he looked okay. He tucked the shirt-tails of his plain black western shirt into his Levi's, grabbed his Gore-Tex jacket and put it on over a sheepskin vest. Not bothering to shave or comb his hair, he left the cabin and headed to the parking area. An hour's drive to the airport was just the thing, anyway, to clear his mind and give him a long draught of freedom.

About seventy minutes later, Alex was standing in a small airport deplaning area, pretty much where Cade Wilder had stood waiting for him four hours earlier. He stood patiently while eight people left the plane, until the attendant shut the exit door. He gave it an extra ten minutes in case the man was still on the plane, even though the plane door had closed. Then he began to worry. Had he missed the visitor? He'd scrutinized every person who'd walked down the ramp, from men in business suits to a Houston man dressed in outlandish cowboy wear. No Scotsman.

He went to the nearest attendant and asked for his man to be called over the PA system. He dug in his shirt pocket for the name Steve had given him: Rory Drummond.

"*Rory Drummond, please meet your party at gate number two.*" The unneeded loudness in the small area was almost amusing. But he'd be damned if he'd screw up and leave the man stranded.

A polite tap on his shoulder, a pleasant husky voice with the soft burr of an accent. "Here is Rory Drummond. Now who could be wanting him?"

He turned to see the man he'd been convinced was a conventioneer from a Houston liquor distributor. A man who seemed to tower over him, dressed in Levi's, gawd-awful high-heel alligator boots, and a shirt with more fringes than a Roy Rogers revival.

He was as tall as Steve Long, probably taller. A good two hundred twenty pounds, all of it muscle, to judge from the way he wore the tight Levi's. His eyes were the kind of green he'd always associated with exotic lagoons. His gold-russet hair lay like a cloud around his face, almost to his shoulders, and he wore a close trimmed beard. Looking at his half-scowl, one side of his upper lip riding his mustache, Alex couldn't tell whether the man was angry, or just confused.

"Mr. Drummond?"

"Aye."

He held out his hand, trying to smile pleasantly and not betray the wicked grin threatening to break out on a face trained to solemnity. "I am Alex Dominguez. I'm your, ah, new hunting partner. Come on, let's stalk your luggage. Then we can relax and talk. Okay?"

The man stood rooted to the spot, looking down into his eyes, his face unreadable. Alex could swear he had the same look on his face as Cade Wilder had worn a few hours earlier. As though looking at him shattered all expectations. For worse or for better? He'd find out.

The man grasped his hand and held it just a little over-long. No doubt the European custom. And when he smiled, his eyes fired with a kind of deep inner glow. Just looking at him made Alex begin to sweat, just a little, in spite of the chill in the room.

So much for the skirt and pom-poms, good holy mother of God. Here stood the most stunningly handsome man he'd ever met.

# Chapter Four
## Of Levi's and Whisky

Walking down the ramp from the blasted plane, Rory felt liberated, yes; but he also felt the effects of jet lag and whisky-laden rumpled sleep. He felt just a hair off-guard, not quite the self-assured man who always took life on like a worthy adversary.

*Maybe it's these foogin Levi's. They ride my crotch, they bite my dick. I need a kilt.* He vowed to strip off the offending trousers as soon as he got to his new base of operations. Whatever and wherever that was.

Thinking about that unknown destination, his scowl disappeared. He'd chosen the place, Long Trails Ranch, based solely on its name and the fact that it was close to a mountain range. He loved the idea of endless trails, where his own feet had consumed too many kilometers to count. Somewhere, Alan Cameron had neatly filed a brochure about the ranch, which he'd actually skimmed over once, a few weeks ago. He vaguely remembered something about "rustic cabins" and "the feel of the wild frontier."

Somehow, being homeless for a while felt like another facet of his strange new liberty. *America. Land of the free. Home of the sodding wild turkey.* He caught himself before he stumbled a little and cursed the new, very narrow cowboy boots. They hurt his feet like a sonofabitch.

In this tiny airport, he managed to miss the man who was supposed to pick him up. Walked straight past him. He was so intent on finding a privy and loosening his balls, he forgot one of the first rules of self-defense: Be aware of your surroundings. He stood at the quaint contraption in the men's privy cupping his own testicles and sighing in relief, thanking God there was no one else there to see a grown man fondling himself in broad daylight.

After taking a piss, Rory bent a little at one of the porcelain basins erected in a neat little row, looking like tiny toilets except too high and too small for a man's bum. He splashed a large amount of cold water on his face and beard, then around the neckline of his new and very wrinkled shirt. He declared himself fit for the hunt ... that hunt being the one for someone, anyone who might be meeting him and carrying him off to a king-sized bed so he could sleep for at least twelve hours.

As soon as he left the privy, he heard own name echoing off the walls of the very small passenger deplaning area. He saw the sign for Gate Two instantly, the same place he'd exited a few minutes ago. And then he stopped as though someone had punched him in the solar plexus. The man standing there, presumably waiting for him, was certainly not a real man, but a foogin dream.

He was tall and slender, with shimmering black hair hanging straight, almost to his shoulders, tucked behind his ears. Somewhat dusky of skin, no doubt Hispanic. He stood with a jacket slung over one very wide shoulder, wearing a sheepskin vest and a dark shirt. His denims seemed painted on, and Rory lavished a long look at the bulge of the crotch. Magnificent.

From the zipper, his eyes traveled to the stranger's face, turned somewhat away from him, and that's when he felt the jolt to his gut. The man had eyes meant to draw angels down to hell, smoky, smoldering, deep.

He adjusted his Levi's, wondering why Americans allowed the world to see their erections so boldly. Without thinking much about his tactic, he worked his way around so that he approached the man from behind. That time-honored technique was his only advantage over one who already had the power to bring him to his knees. Rory thought he might have to muster all his training just so he could manage a conversation with the sexiest man he'd ever laid eyes on.

He barely remembered the man named Alex Dominguez helping him into the oversized vehicle, urging him to strap the seat belt over his large frame, him fumbling like a child, then his new acquaintance finally coming around to stand at his open door while trying to adjust the strap to its fullest extent.

Had he apologized already? He could not remember.

"Sorry, lad. That trip took more out of me than a twenty-kilometer run." As Alex fussed with the strap, Rory caught just a whiff of the man's musky underarm. The aroma of the stranger's maleness, coupled with his nearness, undid him completely, shooting straight to his cock and up his ass. He made no attempt to cover that sudden interest with his hand. Instead, he leaned back on the seat, allowing Alex's forearm to brush his chest while fiddling with the damned seat belt, and looking down he saw his own hard-on and bunched scrotum outlined clearly under the tell-tale denims.

Alex didn't answer. Rory saw that his face had taken on almost a ruby glow, a childlike look of embarrassment mixed with something else. In the brief moments they were so close, he tried to read the expression. Was it veiled excitement? Forced politeness? Or something else? He badly needed to know.

He looked from the man's face to his crotch. The bulge was unmistakable. Even more pronounced than before. Maybe Alex was just naturally well-endowed. His balls began to feel ten kilos heavier, and a dull ache began to crawl from his testes to his prostate.

Alex stepped away, slammed shut the passenger door, and came around to the driver's side, leaning in the window. "You just relax while I load your stuff. It'll take me a minute or two."

*Bloody hell!* He'd forgotten the bags. He would not allow Alex to wipe his ass for one more second, and he unlatched the seat belt, piling out onto the asphalt of the parking lot. "No, no lad. Let me get those."

He stood for a few seconds feeling an unaccustomed confusion. He felt fine, but his actions for the last half hour had been crude, sloppy even. Completely unlike the face he showed to the public. He might stress his gayness in front of his uncle, just to rile the bastard. He might even flaunt his genitals now and then in a frisky game with a willing partner. But here, in the strange atmosphere on the other side of the world, he had become a stranger to himself.

Even as tired as he was, and as besotted by lust, he realized Alex had talked to him from the safe distance of the driver's side window. He would have to "slow his roll," as the expression went. He was a much more restrained man, a far more cultivated man, than his actions betrayed. Alex's tangible embarrassment had now become his own.

He wasn't used to a desirable man backing away from him. He battled with feelings of self-disgust, sexual need, and outright shame. He was aware that those particular emotions were now jumbled together for the first time in his short, happy life.

From five feet away, he stood blocking Alex from picking up the large piece of luggage adorned with bright travel stickers and boarding tags. He was disappointed to see that the man had pulled his jacket down completely over the front of his Levi's.

"No, lad. Really. When I say 'sorry' this time, I want you to understand that I really am rather embarrassed by my own actions. Please forgive me. Honest to God, I am not nearly the lummox you think I am. Let me handle the bag."

Alex looked straight into his eyes, and he felt he was losing his carefully honed public face. There was something about this fine-looking man that demanded honesty. And he had erected so many obstacles to the deep heart of Rory Drummond, he didn't know how to act. Hell, he'd almost forgotten what it was like to tear away the bullshit. He felt his pretenses being peeled away, down to the bone.

"That word *lummox*? I think it means clumsy and stupid. I certainly don't think that, Mr. Drummond. You're jet-lagged, dog tired. Let me lend a hand."

"You take one, I'll take the other. Fair enough?"

The man smiled, one side of his mouth turned in an ironic curl. "Fair enough."

They threw the bags onto the rear-facing seat in the back of the eight-passenger van, and after Alex shut the rear door he turned to him. "We can go back to the ranch now. Or we can find you a decent meal, give you some time to relax before hitting the road. Whaddya think?"

Rory did not have to reflect on it at all. "I want an American steak dinner. A glass of Wild Turkey. And a king-sized bed." *And you, Alex Dominguez, zippered into my skin, your ass gripping my dick from balls to tip.*

Alex laughed a little. "Well ... Steve said I could take you out to dinner and a dance. Guess that'll work out okay. Let's go."

Once back in the passenger seat and snugged in by the simple expediency of his own fingers on the seat belt clasp, Rory leaned back and grinned. "Dinner first, lad. And then the dance."

No sense losing his humor. Not when he'd just found something worth smiling about.

\*\*\*\*

Alex turned at the light outside the airport, then made a left onto Highway 93, heading into Ely. He knew there was a Ramada Inn not too far from Yelland Field. Of course it had a cafe, and maybe the bar would stock Drummond's odd taste in whisky. Who could have guessed a man from Scotland liked an American bourbon?

The man next to him was quiet, his head back as if dozing. Alex could not help stealing a few glances at the large man he'd clearly misjudged. His gaze flicked first to Drummond's face, a study in quiet repose, the eyes closed. Then at his crotch, full to the brim. Hell, he'd have to say *crowded*. The sight made him veer slightly into the breakdown lane, and he managed to right the van without waking his passenger.

*Holy shit. This man is huge in every way. His girth, his height, his personality. His goddamn cock. How in hell am I supposed to spend the next several days yoked to a man who wears his sexuality like a badge of honor?*

He turned into the parking lot of the Ramada Inn, pondering whether he should actually let Rory Drummond check in for the night. Obviously, he was in no shape to take on the cabin waiting for him like a thimble on a thumb. He'd need both cots and maybe another besides just to hold his massive body.

Alex considered the facts of the matter: By the time they got to the ranch, after eating supper and having a few drinks, it would probably be midnight. Dark as a mine. He'd be trying to steer that bear of a man to a place he'd been to just once, through the damn trees, on someone else's property.

He parallel parked outside the office and leaned toward the Scotsman. "Mr. Drummond."

The man cocked his brow and opened one eye. "Are we there yet?"

Alex couldn't help a quick grin. *This guy's a hoot.* "Ah, I'm wondering if you mind checking into the motel tonight. You can go to the ranch tomorrow, early, for breakfast. Our host Steve told me that would be fine with him. Or we can just catch a quick dinner, go to the ranch, about an hour's drive from here."

Drummond righted himself, clearly tired, and shook his head, letting his now-rumpled hair fall somewhat back into place. "Let's check in, lad. I may be able to stumble from the table to a bed. No farther."

The desk clerk inside the small office politely inquired as to the bed arrangements, and the tourist looked at him to translate.

"Um, one bed. Large. The largest you have."

The man behind the desk was young and clearly nervous. Alex considered this might be his first night on the job. He, too, was nervous but trying to put on a bland face. "Mr. Rory Drummond."

The clerk pointed at the place Rory was to sign, and Alex stuck his head out the door to read the license plate of Steve Long's Chevy van. He wrote that, and his own license number, on the motel register, feeling for the first time in his life like a criminal. *No way I'll stay here, not in the same bed with a man I just met. I'll have to come back early tomorrow and pick him up. Shit.*

Drummond opened his passport and copied down the proper identification, dug a bunch of crumpled bills from his pocket, and laid them on the counter. "Ah, keep the change." He grinned at Alex. "A useful expression I learned from the airplane attendants. That way I don't have to piddle with details. Now for a drink and a meal. After you, lad."

Alex couldn't help an answering twitch of his lips, envisioning the oversized Scotsman doling out American currency of unknown worth to doting women in short skirts.

Not bothering to re-park or to haul out the luggage, they walked a ways to the door that read Something-or-other Cafe and went inside.

There were no solicitous waiters, just a large room about a quarter-filled with early diners, and they found a round booth in a corner. As he stripped off his jacket, Alex noticed for the first time that his companion wore no coat of any kind. The overdone cowboy shirt was thin cotton, clearly not much protection from temps that would soon dive into the thirties.

"Did you bring a jacket, Mr. Drummond?"

The Scotsman, already seated, looked up at him with a slight frown. Had he said something to upset the man?

"Look, lad. My name is Rory. And yours is Alex. Let's be friends before we break bread together ... or hoist a glass together. *Comprendes?*"

He slung the jacket across the back of the booth and slid in next to his new friend. The stranger knew enough Spanish to use the familiar ... intimate form of the verb. Something caught fire in his belly. "Fair enough ... Rory."

Rory never did answer his question about the jacket, and Alex decided it was just another way he was trying to wipe the ass of a man who could clearly take care of his own affairs. So he settled down to enjoy the rare occasion of a night out with a very alluring man, one who still made the inside of his thighs buzz whenever he looked at him.

A nice-looking woman in her thirties appeared out of nowhere. "Gentlemen. My name's Rosemary, and I'll be your server. What can I getcha?"

Rory rumbled, "Wild Turkey."

"Come again?"

"Bourbon whisky."

"Oh. Okay. And you, sir?" She turned to Alex with a coquettish tilt to her mouth, and he foolishly ordered whatever his friend was having.

For the next little while, he and the Scotsman traded glasses half-full of something resembling whisky. A cross between scotch and diesel fuel, a brand he'd never heard of. Dinner was still a long way off, but he found himself not caring at all.

By the time they ordered their steaks, they were sitting about a foot apart, not too close. Not close enough to raise eyebrows. Alex remembered being twice that distance apart when he'd first sat down, but somehow he didn't give a shit.

When their dinner finally arrived, some kind of meat that could have been steak, they both ate as though it were the finest prime rib. At one point, Rory lifted his head and jabbed him with a strange look.

"Those eyes."

"What?"

"A man could drown in them."

The way he said it ... raw, direct, unsmiling ... caught him off guard. Alex drew in a sharp breath at the same time blood pumped into his cock first, then spread, a wildfire, consuming every inch of his body. He felt the heat rise even to his neck and into his ears. He and the other man seemed to lock eyes for long minutes, but it must have been seconds before he ducked his head to stare at the dinner plate. When he dared to glance up again, the Scotsman was calmly eating, looking around at the surroundings, fingering his whisky glass.

He must have heard it wrong. The Scottish accent, his way of quirking one side of his upper lip into his mustache, his own desperate longing... Alex kept eating in silence, aware that the conversation had failed miserably. He tried to pick it back up, straighten the ragged edges.

"So ... tell me about your flight."

"Why is it, lad, everyone always asks about the most miserable part of any trip? I haven't a foogin idea. I was drunk the whole way. And now, at last, I'm in my own private heaven."

He was almost afraid to ask, because Rory was setting him up for it. "And what heaven is that?"

So quickly he didn't see it coming, the handsome man leaned closer and put his lips close to his ear, almost touching the delicate rim. The heat of his breath sent a jumping, jolting current under his skin that traveled all the way up his ass. God in heaven what was this man doing? And why wasn't he, Alex, leaning away from almost tasting his breath?

"A perfect dinner companion. One who fires my ... imagination."

He straightened up again and grinned. "Worry not, Alex. I can hold my whisky, but by God I'd rather not right now. I'll answer you truthfully. My heaven is right here. The freedom to breathe at last, free of constraints. No one cocking an eyebrow at my decisions, questioning my choices. No one taking stock of whether I chose the right kilt for the weather."

The man leveled his deep green eyes again into his own. "I have a question for you. What is it you most enjoy doing?"

"I ... suppose ... working out. Walking. Feeling the miles under my feet."

"Alex, that sounds like a lonesome kind of pleasure. No faithful companion? A sweetheart? Maybe a wife?"

The Scotsman was so blatantly open, so charmingly naive in his question, Alex could not help showing a rare smile. "None of the above."

Again the eyes probed his. "Unbelievable. Yet some men would rather be left alone. I understand, lad."

Was Rory setting him up for a denial? Because he wanted to shout, *No, I want someone to fuck my ass, fuck my mouth, take me into his private heaven ... I want you, Rory Drummond.*

"I didn't say I preferred the loneliness. That's just the way my life is going right now."

"Well, we have each other for a week. Perhaps your heaven and mine will intersect."

Flustered again, Alex looked away, and Rory put a hand lightly on his forearm. "I mean we might hike a trail together, you and I. Another of life's rare pleasures."

In spite of himself, Alex smiled. Rory was a comical mix of naive and subtle, naughty boy and sexy man. Suddenly his onerous assignment felt a lot lighter. *Maybe this man will end up babysitting me instead. Christ in heaven, I hope so.*

When they left, it was into a bitter cold night, but Alex was hardly feeling it. They sort of walked together to room 13B. Rory slid a magnetic card in the door slot and stood aside. "After you, lad."

He stood for a moment inside the room watching the sliver of light between the tiny overhead fixture outside and the black interior where he found himself, scared shitless at his own bold decision. His new friend closed the door, not bothering to flick on the light. His next sensation was a still-hungry mouth seeking the tender skin under his chin, teeth gnawing his throat, his lips, and the sound of a moan slow-bleeding into the dark. It was his own soft cry, and for once in his life he didn't give a shit when he plunged his tongue into a blessed wetness, fucked the man's downy-whiskered mouth, accepted his tightening embrace, allowed himself to be picked up and carried to a place of release.

# Chapter Five
## To the Core

**R**ory had to admit, he'd fucked dozens of men. Big, small, and in-between ... and that was their cocks, not their height and weight. He'd taken weak and strong, burly and thin. He'd seduced young sprouts, those his own age, men much older than himself. Rich and poor, educated and non. Now, for the first time, he emphatically wanted not to fuck. He wanted to make love. If only his whisky-riddled body would allow it.

He could not explain to himself why this reticent young man—a serious stranger not bent on finding a sex partner—why Alex should have roped him and pulled him in like he had. Was it the man's very reluctance to admit his attraction? Could it be the passionate eyes, promising more than Alex could possibly realize? Whatever it was, Rory had never felt like this before. He was not simply attracted. He needed Alex Rodriguez at a level which might have scared him, he admitted, if he weren't so bloody drunk.

The man he carried in the black night of a foreign place was almost as large as himself. And yet, in spite of the bulk in his arms and his pinched feet in the cowboy boots, he strode easily to an unseen bed, never loosening his mouth from Alex's insistent hold, sucking a tongue threatening to choke him.

In a few steps, his knees felt the edge of a bed. He bent and laid his new lover on the surface. He wanted light, he wanted to watch that mobile face as he undressed him, needed to see those eyes that had rendered him helpless from the moment he'd jumped in and was drowned in a riptide.

He heard his own voice, rough with passion, as his lips traced the delicate edge of his ear. "Don't move. Never go away." He'd been in so many hostels, inns, hotels and other places of one-night relief that he knew he had only to roll a little and grope for a night stand. He did that, and found the push button on the bedside lamp. At a touch, pale light revealed his partner lying in his jacket and vest, trousers and hiker's boots.

Alex was staring up at him, silent. Rory saw his chest rise and fall, ragged, uncontrolled. His eyes were pools of dark lust. He twisted his head, shut his eyes, and Rory saw the man try to swallow, then gasp, try again. "I can't—"

Rory bent over Alex, cupped his face, again lowered his mouth and let his lips move on his lover's. "Yes, yes, Alex. *Alejo mio*. You can, we can. Let me undress you."

First he kicked off his own bloody boots. Still in the uncomfortable Levi's, he took a few minutes to peel them off and to strip the shirt too, unmindful of buttons, his fingers becoming tangled in the goddamn tassels that hung everywhere, undulating in tune with the blood pumping and pounding in his cock. He straddled Alex with naked thighs burning to touch flesh to flesh.

Removing the jacket, then the vest, he talked his way down the shirt front. "I am not ... a nimble-fingered man ... when it comes to foogin buttons and seat belts." Christ, the man had a chest the envy of any martial artist he'd ever encountered. The swells of his breasts, the peaks of the strawberry nipples, demanded his mouth. And so he bent and began to nip and pull, bite and lick, his erection feeding on the grunts and moans Alex was trying to suppress.

The metal button on the Levi's finally yielded to his clumsy attempts, then the bloody zipper. He pulled the offending trousers down, met the resistance of his boots. *Bloody hell!* He somehow unlaced and removed the Timberlands, then pulled the Levi's off completely. Still riding him as though he were a wild horse, Rory paused to admire the man beneath his pinioning thighs.

Alex's hips were moving in the ageless rhythm of ungratified need. And his thick wedge of a cock was stiff, purpled. Needing him. The man still said nothing, but the canyons of his eyes begged for satisfaction, his mouth moved with inarticulate longing, every inch of his superb body screamed for release.

Rory tasted the cheap whisky churning in his gut, grateful it was slowing him down. Because on a normal day, with a foogin devil of an angel trapped under his thighs, he might have fountained already just looking at the high cheekbones and full, sulky mouth of an impossibly sexy lover. Even altogether drunk, he felt a ragged electric charge skip along every nerve, threatening to make him spill his cum, just watching Alex mouth his name.

His eyes traveled from the face, down the long throat, past the wide shoulders to the chest matted with curling black hair. And the treasure trail, dark, ending in a wedge of thick black pubic hair … Lust coated the inside of his mouth, spread even to his fingertips, crowded out every thought except the unholy thrill of emptying his seed into this man.

What kind of training did Alex have, that every muscle stood as though hewn by a chisel? The long, ropy veins of his shoulders and arms revealed hidden strength under a skin so transparent as to be creamy brown porcelain. If this man wanted, he could be a formidable match in any confrontation. And this one was no exception. *Will you fight me, Alex lad, or yield to me, let me come inside you?*

He knew there would be no lubricant tonight. The gel and condoms were tucked away in his luggage, bugger his own lack of imagination for letting that happen. Only one way to grease his passage, the way he preferred in any case. He eased his bulk from Alex and knelt between his legs.

He pushed both his lover's legs up until the knees were bent, then slid his hands under the firm buttocks, lifting his entire groin to his starving mouth. He started with the cock itself, licking and slavering, relaxing his throat to take in as much as possible.

A strangled cry told him Alex loved what he was doing, and the music of his lover's passion set a rhythm to his mouth. Up and down the shaft, around the thick cowl, to the balls, whisking them almost down his throat, then releasing them in bubbles of spit. Christ, Mary and all the saints of heaven, he was in danger of coming as he let his fingers probe the entrance to the asshole, feeling his own discharge seep from the slit of his cock, quicksilver burning a hole to his core.

First one finger, then two. Spreading them and scissoring, he opened Alex more and more. "*Rory...*" Three fingers, then four, into a chasm that immediately closed around his flesh as he withdrew, then opened as he pushed in again. "*Rory, I need...*"

He lifted Alex's entire groin to his mouth, nosed his balls aside, and sought the opening nestled deep in his crack.

As soon as his mouth found the pliable hole, he spread Alex's ass and began to thrust his tongue, deeply and wetly, leaving as much spittle as possible. By now his lover was almost out of control, and he had to grip the buttocks hard while he tongue-fucked and slobbered, spit and licked.

The moment had come. The hole was loose, soaking wet, and the firecracker up his own ass was ready to explode. He straddled Alex again, leaning close to his head. "Keep your knees up, laddie, as far as you can, over my shoulders."

He heard Alex sobbing, heard his own deep moan of need, guided his cock to the wet entrance. *Push, push against unyielding flesh and keep thrusting* ... until the miracle of manlove happened and the bunched knot gave way to a sliding, hot frenzy of moving muscle.

When he felt his entire being slide to the core, he leaned into Alex's mouth. "Let me in all the way, *Alejo, mi Alejo.*" His tongue and cock both felt a scalding heat as he pumped and moaned, needing to come, yet needing to satisfy his lover too. "Come, please come, Alejo."

As he spoke, he felt the spasms begin, a grabbing on his cock that told him the man was starting a deep orgasm. Needing no more, he lost all control, his own flesh tearing into the endless volcanic hole of Alex Dominguez. And then the flooding, the final release, a ripping apart of his soul when the cum shot into his lover's pulsing ass.

He lay there for what seemed ten minutes, even longer. He felt Alex's strong arms around his chest and burrowed ever inward, to the source of unending solace. He felt his lover's warm cum on his belly and tried to sink into it, too, loving the fact that he'd given pleasure to this man.

When he finally rolled, it was only a little to the side so he could still feel Alex's arms around him, pulling him close. Fighting to stay awake he began to kiss him again, this time very slow and deliberate, sensitive to every touch. He was not aware of sliding into sleep, only a moving against his lips as Alex murmured something that sounded like *fuck me forever*.

\*\*\*\*

Rory Drummond lay in his arms, a hulk of a man become a young boy nesting against his chest, one arm still circling his shoulder. His deep breathing and the thrum of a snore somewhere in his throat told Alex his lover was deep in sleep, completely drained of everything but sour whisky.

*Is this any way to start my new job?*

A cramp in his stomach answered his own question. *I've betrayed the governor already. A few hours after meeting my assigned man, I've fallen ass over prick for him.*

He looked closely at Rory, loving the way his mouth, now relaxed, seemed to be savoring the aftertaste of their kissing. *His cum is still lodged up my ass.* For some reason, that thought made his depleted cock move feebly, trying to wake, and he swore softly against Rory's steel-hard arm. He knew his own ejaculate was smeared on both their bellies, now become a kind of glue welding the two of them.

*Madre de Diós*, he'd just experienced the first real fuck of his life. Instead of a clumsy blowjob, or a hasty poking into his ass by some anonymous desperate prick, he had actually been fucked. Made love to, really. And from the goddamn front, like a man would take a woman. Except it was anything but.

The experience had been completely masculine, deeply sexy, wholly satisfying. The orgasm had started not in his balls but well inside his ass, so far up he still felt a faint flutter of muscle excitement all along his channel when he least expected the thrill to flare again.

He lay there at least half an hour, knowing they could sleep only a few hours before having to meet the pre-dawn, drive to the ranch, face strangers across a breakfast table. The more he tried to shut out Rory's love-making, the more wide awake he felt.

How ironic. The man he'd imagined in a girly skirt with a ridiculous cap had just fucked the holy crap out of him, and he wanted it all over again. The man he was supposed to keep out of trouble had stuffed his oversized prick into the place where all hell had broken out.

Thinking about the intense ride up his asshole, his cock wakened fully, wanting to exact a ransom, needing to find its own refuge in his lover's crack and beyond. He pulled Rory closer, hoping to rouse him without really waking him. "Turn over, man." He licked the man's ear, then pushed his tongue softly inside. "Let me take you."

He could not explain to himself why he wanted this man, this impossible mountain of flesh and cheeky, unashamed horniness. He had a feeling Rory was a very accomplished purveyor of sexual favors, one who'd no doubt fucked men from paupers to princes and everyone in between. There was a certain ... youth and exuberance, a kind of childlike charm in his manner that held Alex in a state of breathless expectation. Excitement, even. *Face it, Alex. Complete, fucking arousal.*

As if hearing his whispered command, Rory turned over heavily, nesting his ass in the curve of his groin. He could still hear the rhythmic soft snores, and that gave him the courage to spit on his fingers and apply the saliva to his cock. Again and again, he fingered his own prick, coating it with spit, letting his fingers play along the length, imagining them to be Rory's own, playing him like an instrument.

He moved away a little, balanced on one elbow, concentrating on a pair of well-shaped buttocks in the dim lamplight, mounds of muscle laid over with satin flesh. Again his prick leapt with anticipation, and he hoisted one leg across his back, set his tip in the crack, forced the cheeks apart, hoping his lover would wake ... but slowly. He wanted Rory to wake with the reality of steel riding his asshole and push back, open wide, let him in all the way.

Alex knew he was far too reserved to initiate the sex act. Only with a lover half-assed asleep did he dare to begin the subtle, slow push inside. Then out again. Wet his prick, thrust in once more. And it happened. Instead of a wall of resistance, Rory's asshole seemed to flare like the head of a cobra, widen and snap shut on his cock, as he slid in and out, up and down.

He heard a groan, maybe his own, and set up a rhythmic dance, a plunging and retreating that leapt and jumped like a dervish in his blood. He was not imagining it. Rory's ass had begun to fist and let go, open and close on his dick while he lost all inhibitions and began to tell him how he felt.

"I love it ... Rory ... I need to fuck you. Now, now. God, let me come..."

The pulses on his cock were now a goddamn squeezing, a relentless hold and release, and Rory's feral cry fired him to climax: "Come, Alejo... Damn it, come in me." He felt a shuddering release, a sluicing of his semen into pure blessed heat, into a hole that opened then closed on his sputtering prick, exacting its own kind of ransom.

Afterwards, he lay with his head against Rory's massive back, listening to the soft burr of his renewed snore, wishing he could stay there the rest of his life, knowing he was drifting into an impossible dream.

Alex woke with the conviction that it was time to leave. He managed to extract his watch hand from beneath his bed-mate and read the luminous dial. Four-ten. Steve would expect them by six. *Fuck*. He sat up and looked at his bed companion. Sprawled like a kid, Rory took up three-fourths of a king-sized bed. He wanted to snug next to the man, wake him with a long tongue somewhere or other, but his better judgment prevailed.

He slid from the bed, found his rumpled clothes on the floor, and hung them half-assedly from a chair sitting against the wall. For the first time, he looked around at the room that had heard his whimpers and howls of lust. Completely cookie-cutter, it was no more than a bed with matching nightstands and lamps, two chairs, one large dresser and three doors. One was the entrance, one was no doubt a closet, and the last would be a blessed toilet and tub.

He opened the second door, sure enough a tiny closet, then opened the other. Standing at the toilet, he released what seemed an unending stream of piss, grateful to relieve his bladder of some of the poison he'd drunk last night. As he took a wiz, he eyed the tub-shower combo, knowing this would be the last time in several days he and his companion would have the luxury of a hot bath or shower.

He flicked his prick and walked to the shower, seriously debating whether to cleanse himself now or wait for Rory. His companion no doubt needed the sleep. Maybe he could wait just a little before waking him. *Rory will need a change of clothes.* He went back to the bedroom and drew on his jeans and shirt, pulled on the boots, and quickly shouldered into the jacket. Extracting the keys from his pocket and the motel card from the side table, he went outside to meet the stabbing cold of a mid-fall morning in the foothills of Eastern Nevada.

The snap of bitter cold on his eyeballs told him temps were maybe in the upper twenties. He quickly walked to the Chevy van and opened the rear, hauled out Rory's two large bags, and finally made it back to the door of 13B. Damn, the man must carry a sled dog around with him to go with the fucking toboggan.

He smiled at his own stupid image, knowing a sled dog did not pull that kind of contraption, and opened the door, throwing in the bags one after the other. He closed it quickly, already chilled to the bone.

Looking toward the bed, expecting to see the mound of a man, he saw an empty room. He heard the sound of running water and realized Rory was already in the shower. Once in the bathroom, his offending clothes on the floor, he saw the outline of his lover's flesh bump against the semi-sheer shower curtain. He filled his lungs with a huge intake of air, daring to be bold for once, and parted the curtain.

Seeing the man now in the overhead light, his heart began to batter his ribcage again. The pulsing water ran down a body so muscled he thought he himself must look like a Boy Scout in comparison. Rivulets streamed from his hair to his shoulders, caught and eddied in the planes of his abdomen and his navel, then pooled and beaded in his russet groin hairs. The cock rose from that nest of hair, an eagle in flight from its aerie. Alex's imagination soared right along with Rory's magnificent phallus.

The man flashed a disarming smile. "Obviously I've been thinking about you, lad."

Suddenly embarrassed, Alex ducked his head a little and held out his hand for the bar of soap in Rory's hand.

"Soap, man. I need soap. Everywhere, and fast."

"Stand there, Alex. I'll do the honors."

Still flustered, he turned his back to Rory, allowing him to run soapy hands from his head all the way past the inside of his knees, down to this feet. On the way back up, his fingers slid along his crack, and his mouth nestled in his ear. "Damn, Alex. They say the third time's the charm."

He turned around, now completely flummoxed, knowing his cock had reared again. And suddenly knowing Rory had not been asleep at all during that second Taking of Scotland.

"Enough, man. Just soap me."

Rory lathered him while stroking his mouth with his tongue, running the bar between his legs, over his balls, up his cock, then into his ass for good measure. "I think our mountain retreat will not boast a hot shower. Am I right?"

Trying to wrest his head away, needing to restore some shred of his former self-control, he spoke into his lover's busy mouth. "Yes."

"Then come here, Alex. I want you all over again."

Rory picked him up by the buttocks, spreading his cheeks, and set his asshole squarely on top of his mountain of a cock, already lathered and ready. He slipped in easily, greedily, while the big man raised him up and down, all the while flaying his lips and licking the flesh of his throat.

"Never ... never a lover so sexy... I need all of you." Rory murmured and whispered while Alex ejaculated, hard, feeling the spasms in his rectum seize Rory's flesh and rock the entire inside of his shaking ass.

By the time his lover released him, Alex was absolutely ready to lock the motel room door and throw the fucking key down the toilet.

# Chapter Six
## Summit and Valley

He was living an impossible dream at the moment, Rory knew. The crisp fall air, the scenery drifting into forever until it met a razorback mountain chain. The infinite expanse of cloudless sky, a land of raw promise. If he possessed no more than that, he would count himself a man more fortunate than most.

But now he had Alex. A man so sexy, so beguiling, he still felt like a bloody adolescent in his presence. He was not merely blessed. Fate had handed him an angel, and he hardly knew how to contain his joy or his arousal either.

Sitting next to the quiet man maneuvering the oversized vehicle, watching the dark curling ribbon of highway slowly become a straight path to the distant mountains as the predawn painted the sky, he settled back in a kind of blissful stupor, thinking about their evening together.

It was clear to him that Alex was not seasoned in the ageless game of sexual delight. In spite of his jaw-dropping looks, the man wore his naiveté as guilelessly as those tight trousers. From their first half hour together yesterday, Rory had delighted in the way his new lover stole glances at him through lowered eyelids, thinking he didn't notice. Each time Alex pretended not to look at his crotch, Rory's erection grew more adamantine.

*Christ, the man turns me inside out. And those foogin eyes...*

He was besotted with the man, his cock restless with the need to penetrate that tight ass again and again. He responded deeply to Alex's unvarnished need, his unaffected desperation for a real lover to possess him. Last night, when Alex had half-assed straddled him from behind and entered him, he'd pretended grogginess and let him be the alpha. And by God, with only a little goading, he was convinced they could be equals in bed. They could and would fight for cock o' the walk. He'd work on that starting five minutes ago.

They had just come over a stretch of winding highway called Connors Summit, a mountain pass he knew could be treacherous in bad weather. Alex handled the van easily, letting the descent from the summit feel to his stomach like a small plane doing loop-the-loops while maintaining utter control of the vehicle. When the road straightened into a vast valley, he spoke into the silence which had prevailed the last ten minutes. "You seem to like being in the driver's seat, lad."

A tick of silence. "Meaning?"

"Meaning nothing. Merely an observation. You seem relaxed, sure of yourself..." He didn't add the obvious ... *instead of a boy finding hairs in his crotch for the first time.* Like last night. It wouldn't be fair to judge Alex that way. His very inexperience was part of what most attracted Rory. That, and his undeniable sensuality, a power that emanated from some bottomless source in his character.

"I guess I didn't tell you, Rory. I'm a Nevada State Trooper. Ah, kind of a kindergarten cop, lowest rung of law enforcement. My job is to sit behind a wheel all day. Scout the highways, look for speeders and drunks. If I didn't like being in the driver's seat, God knows what other line of work I'd be in. A big rig driver maybe? Anyway, being here settles my soul, kind of."

Rory let that sink in. The man was a policeman. No wonder he had that look of caution, a way of walking and moving that didn't give away his hidden power. Except for those broad shoulders, he hid his build and strength on purpose. The revelation fired him to the marrow, set his blood to pumping faster. He felt like he was diving off that summit head first.

He couldn't help asking, "What's a big rig?"

"A Rory Drummond with eighteen wheels."

The witty answer just about finished him off, accelerating his skydive into slap-happy.

He felt like his persistent grin had begun to split and crack his cheeks. "And how is it, lad, that a policeman gets a holiday?"

He saw Alex glance over at him a second before settling his remarkable eyes back on the front windshield. "Even a cop can take time off, Rory. This valley, these mountains ... they're part of my growing up. Coming back here is a kind of homecoming for me."

"Tell me."

"Um, a little later. I promise to tell you, okay? I'd rather know more about you. Why you chose this state, these mountains, over any other place in the world."

"That's simple, Alex. I haven't actually studied Nevada. But it's always fascinated me. Did you know the good Lord could drop four Scotlands into Nevada? I studied archaeology in school, some mineralogy and even geography. Nevada's a natural attraction. And the history of this place fascinates me too. The ghost towns, the Indian artifacts, the silver mining. So why not? I love the mountains and open spaces. This is heaven for me."

His driver let a few seconds tick by. "So you and I will have a lot to talk about on those lonely hikes you promised." Again Alex stole a look at him, this time with a crooked smile, and Rory's stomach did a somersault as though they were still coming off that summit.

"Tell me where we're going, lad. And why you called me your hunting partner."

"Well. The headquarters is a place called Long Trails Ranch. Which I'm sure you know already. It's named after a man, Steve Long. I met him yesterday. His ranch is not a total working ranch, like the rest in Snake Valley. He's devoted his resources to taking folks on big game hunts. A few in the fall, mostly for mule deer. Others in the spring ... fishing, bird shooting. Told me he used to work in these mountains, what they call a game warden, making sure the land stays pristine, helping to manage the wildlife, looking for poachers, that kind of thing."

"Of course. Even we primitives in Scotland have our forest wardens. Impressive. So the man must know what he's doing. How is it you call me your partner? I'm flattered, naturally, lad, but we hardly know each other."

This time when Alex looked over at him, the reticent man was wearing a delighted smile. "He calls it the 'buddy system.' He pairs off the guests, makes us responsible for each other's well-being. I have your back, you have mine."

"Foogin right, lad. What I want most."

He watched a dull flush rise from Alex's neck to his cheeks and felt his own cock rise up and shout for assistance. He hadn't even intended the double meaning, had just now caught his own unintended jest, but Alex had understood it immediately.

"I mean, Alex ... that's ingenious. A way of making sure grown men don't shoot their own peckers off."

Alex laughed outright, and Rory loved the sound. It was fresh, spontaneous, warm, and he began to feel a kind of dizzy rapture utterly new to him. *This man has already dug under my thick skin, heading straight to a place that may not be ready to shelter him.* And now he felt a burning on his own cheeks, another sensation that was alien to him.

They turned at a junction sign, where the road ahead was known as "Fifty-slash-Six." Alex told him Highway 50 would give way to Highway Six somewhere in Utah, east over the stretch of mountains called the Snake Range.

"And this valley, Rory? It's known as Snake Valley. A place that wants water more than anything else. Even so, it holds a cruel beauty, no different from the reptile itself. Like thirst on the edge of starvation, but still inside heaven's gates. If that makes any sense."

Rory looked at the valley unfolding before him, now caught in the first light. It seemed almost purple and gold, like a piece of agate with undulating bands of subtle color. And rising from the valley floor a range of mountains higher than any he'd ever beheld. The sun beginning to rise from their ragged outline shone on a sparkling crust of ice and snow, sending scintillations of light back to the vast sky.

"Heaven. Aye, lad. I feel it to the heart of me."

Alex would figure he was talking about the scene in front of them. He didn't see Rory turn his head to look directly at the driver, not the valley. He didn't know Rory's words were also about him. A man who'd begun to steal into his core and nest there, a fledgling eagle, not yet ready to spread its wings and fly away.

****

Coming back into Snake Valley, letting the speed and movement of the van settle under his ass, Alex felt an odd contentment. Not the same as when he made his patrols, his hard gaze ever watchful for the unexpected. Now his eyes kept turning to the magnetic man who sat next to him. Sometimes he merely glanced, hoping Rory didn't guess at his unbounded attraction. Other times, he outright turned his head and met his eyes, those tide pools of sensuous promise.

The dashboard clock read 5:35. Plenty of time to drive to the ranch and unload before piling into the house to meet and greet. He found himself looking forward to introducing Rory, like showing the ball-goers the emperor's crown. In spite of himself, he smiled.

"A crowned thistle for your thoughts, lad?"

"Say what?"

His companion chuckled. "You sound like our fair Rosemary when I asked for Wild Turkey. A crowned thistle is a five-pence coin. The Queen's nod to my bonnie country."

"I forgot already why I was smiling. Something about an emperor's crown..." He did remember, of course. No sense confessing to Rory how fascinating he already seemed to him. The man was completely down-to-earth, would never tolerate another man talking like a schoolgirl with a crush.

The closer he drew to the ranch, the more his eyes sought Moriah. He knew in the days to come how his father's very breath would seem to sigh through the canyons, how every sight would take him to a time of innocence and unbounded freedom. And now he'd be revisiting his father with a companion. In a sense, bringing Rory to meet him, to ask his blessing...

His mind snapped shut on the furtive thought. He was here to hunt, period. They'd probably not come within half a mountain of his old stomping grounds. He saw the sign telling them the Long Trails Ranch lay one half mile ahead, and he steered the van onto the side road, letting the uneven road pepper his ass with jolts and talk rough to his vulnerable balls as the rocky surface jarred with the Chevy's suspension.

For the millionth time he stole a glance at Rory, sitting straight with anticipation, his dark blue flannel shirt almost bursting with the muscles that pulled at its seams. The cowboy shirt had become a wrinkled ball of fringes, stuffed back into his luggage, forgotten. With the new shirt, and his tight Levi's, Rory could almost pass for a native. Except for the alligator skin boots he insisted on wearing.

Alex suppressed a smile. When the blisters grew big enough, those freaking boots would be buried with the tasseled shirt.

He swung onto the ranch house grounds, taking the wide, curved drive-up nice and slow, suddenly reluctant to share Rory with anyone else. If they were lucky, they'd be able to unload the luggage in their assigned cabin and walk to the house for breakfast without disturbing any of the ranch hands. Besides, he badly wanted to be alone with Rory for just thirty seconds. Long enough to feel himself being drawn close to that large hard body, feel his mouth ransacked and his ass fired all the way to his bellybutton.

"C'mon, Rory. Let's hunt the wild cabin." He parked the van as close as he could to their small building and hopped out. Going around back to extract the bags, he met Rory on the other side of the rear door. They stood very close for a few seconds, Rory raking his eyes with his dangerous green tidewater, Alex feeling his cock bang against the goddamn zipper of his jeans.

Without a word, each seized one of Rory's bags. Together, they walked through the sparse stand of trees, down a graveled walkway, and into the thicker copse of mesquite and pine that shielded their cabin.

Alex dropped the luggage and fished for the door key. It was a simple large key, to fit a simple rustic lock. When he'd opened the door, he stood rock still. Rory looked at him in surprise.

"What?"

"After you, Mr. Drummond."

It was his deliberate way of reminding both of them about their entry last night into the motel room. Except now it was reversed. A tiny gesture that set Rory's eyes smoldering and had Alex's own prick crying for immediate freedom from his freaking Levi's.

As soon as Rory stepped inside, Alex bent and picked up the pieces of luggage. One by one he set them inside the door while his companion waited, this time not insisting on helping. Once inside, he turned around and latched the door.

Before he even swiveled around, Rory was behind him, his hard crotch riding the small of his back and his hands tight around his midsection. A brushing on his ear of soft beard, a husky murmur in his ear, "I need you," and Alex was already shaking with suppressed desire.

When Rory began to bite the side of his neck under the ear, he managed to laugh and turn in his arms. "We'll be late—"

A sliding and slipping of tongues ... sounds of ravening hunger, bubbles of spit and greed... Both of their mouths were unstoppable, insatiable, their hands running roughshod over the other man's crotch and ass, undeterred by the stiff denim.

"By God, lad, I'll have you now. Breakfast can wait."

"No." He pulled away forcibly from Rory's lumberjack arms. "Rory. We have a lot of time to, um, be together. Now we're guests of another man. Let's respect that."

Rory surprised him by standing back immediately.

"Of course. I forgot myself. Will you forgive me?"

The humongous man looked so contrite, so almost childlike, Alex reached one hand to his soft beard and stroked, letting his fingers end on Rory's expressive wide mouth. "There's nothing to forgive."

When his lover immediately caught his fingers up in his passionate mouth and began to suck, Alex lowered his hand and grinned. "Breakfast now, fingers later. Okay?"

"Anything you say, Alex. Lead the way. I'm starved, but not for foogin breakfast."

# Chapter Seven
## Family

**B**reakfast was a triumph, in Rory's estimation. Not just the manna Americans called "flapjacks," soft cakes soaked in butter and sweet maple syrup, nor even the crisp bacon and scrambled eggs he savored. No, the simple meal was made a celebration by the presence of Alex and a handful of rugged, handsome men who tucked in their chins and simply ate.

He looked around as he contentedly chewed, watching his new acquaintances, starting at the head of the long cedar-plank table. Steve Long, owner and guide, was big as his name. An absolutely long man, almost his height, with a head of dark hair he rumpled back from his forehead now and again, making him look even longer. Crystalline blue eyes that saw everything. Rory was convinced that from the moment that man looked from him to Alex, he knew ... or guessed ... their more-than-buddies relationship.

Next to Steve sat his head man, what he called a "wrangler," one he'd introduced simply as Jack. He estimated Jack to be in his early fifties, his father's age, with a body that men half his age should envy—lean, muscled, disciplined in movement even when forking flapjacks onto his plate.

At Steve's other elbow hunkered a leathery-faced man not nearly so old as his sun-weathered skin, mid-thirties maybe, another wrangler named Zeb. He was shoveling in food while his sharp eyes took in every nuance of the clipped conversation around him. Both those men carried an air of quiet competence. When they spoke, it was in short bursts, as though the language itself was precious enough to dole out piece by piece.

Alex sat next to him, their arms almost touching; and across from his lover was the cook Paul, a forty-ish slender man with merry eyes and an old-fashioned handlebar mustache.

"Rest of the boys ate already?" Steve was addressing his cook, who nodded, mouth full. He looked at Rory and offered an unnecessary explanation. "This ranch keeps about ten men. Looking after the horses and cattle, helping on the expeditions. Every one of 'em keeps me upright and moving ahead. Thank God for good men."

Rory smiled. "Amen."

"Tell us a little about you, Rory." Steve had put down his fork and was regarding him with eyes that Rory swore could pick apart blarney and call it crap. Not unfriendly. Just watchful, calculating.

"Lad, I am bloody boring, next to any one of you. I run a small castle, probably about the same square footage as your ranch holdings. In fact, I don't even run it. Like you, I depend on good men, and a few lasses too, otherwise I'd no doubt give in to my wanderlust and just hit the road. Or the mountain trail."

"Oh? You live near mountains?"

Rory took some time to talk about his Cairngorms, Scotland's answer to Steve's own Snake Range. "Not so dramatic as yours. After all, we're only scant miles from the sea. But rugged. Northern face snow-clad most of the year. Endlessly fair, angels with ... with pure white hair." He was suddenly embarrassed at his flight of fancy, but every man at the table nodded in understanding.

Jack looked up from his plate. "You hunt, Rory?"

"I do, lad. In Scotland, we call it 'stalking.' Deerstalking, mostly mulies. But also bear, elk, moose ... whatever the season calls for."

"Shit, Rory, you have us all beat." Zeb was grinning at him, using his fork to punctuate his words. "What kind of rifle?"

"Medium to long range. Give me a Ruger, boys, the finest I've ever used."

What were once grunts turned into an earnest discussion of the merits of Ruger versus Remington versus Browning. Short range versus medium and long. Scopes and ammo. Even Alex, who'd mostly been listening, agreed with Rory and Zeb on the Ruger long-range.

After a while Rory sat back and listened to his new acquaintances, already almost a family, feeling the excitement of the hunt begin to ride up his shoulder blades, as it always did. He noticed that Steve, too, merely listened while seeming to do no more than eat. The man was one he'd like to know better. In spite of the man's undeniable good looks, he felt no stir of his cock, only a genuine interest in him as a fellow hunter, a ranch-manager and a human being.

Rory's wild-ass choice of ranch based simply on a whimsical name might turn out to be the most important choice of his life. Now it was his turn to steal a look at his partner, elbows on the table, leaning forward to lend his opinion of tracking techniques. The light blue of his shirt seemed to pool back in his lively dark eyes, and Rory made an effort to look beyond the man, to the room they sat in.

From what he could tell, the entire ranch house was simple, sturdy, and comfortable. Indian rugs hung from the walls in this room, and a few collections of handsome Indian artifacts were arranged in shadow boxes: arrowheads, spear points, small axe heads. He wanted to study each one, delight in the proximity to something he'd seen only in books; yet he was loath to leave the convivial table.

"Rory."

Steve's quiet voice made him pivot his head in answer.

"Your accommodations ... are they okay?"

"I'll be honest, Steve. Alex and I walked in and right back out again. I haven't even unpacked yet."

"Be sure to let me know if there's something you need."

"I will, lad. There's something I don't need ... but I want. Something I won't find here on the ranch." He was almost hesitant to bring it up. But his host had asked. When Steve raised his brows, he continued. "I couldn't find a cowboy hat in Scotland. I'd like to buy one before we leave on the hunt."

Steve grinned for the first time, a smile that changed his entire face, made the man ten years his senior seem like a kid. "A what? Not an item anyone here would wear, except my wranglers. No use on a hunt, especially on the heads of first-timers."

Every word Steve spoke made the hat more desirable than ever. "Maybe you'll let me ride one of your horses. With my new cowboy hat, my Levi's and boots, you might even hire me on as a wrangler."

Steve stood, laughing out loud. "I probably would, Rory. You go ahead and buy that hat. Warren's Western Wear in Ely would carry something in your size. Maybe. You're one big fella."

Alex stood too. "Could we, um ... use the van?" He seemed embarrassed to ask, but Steve just grinned. "Keep those keys, Alex. You can even be my official chauffeur for the guests coming in tomorrow. Perfect."

They walked together back to the cabin, both silent. Rory thought Alex seemed happy, judging from the easy way he carried himself, the small smile playing around the corners of his mouth.

The smile piqued more than his interest. "What?"

Alex glanced up at him. "Let's make a pact to get our clothes out of our luggage and hung up before ... before we go back into town."

Rory felt the twinge of need, running from his cock through his balls and down his thighs. Prickles of excitement jumped from his scrotum to his asshole, playing games with his most private skin. His voice sounded a little rough to his own ears. "Aye. Promise. Clothes first." They reached the cabin and paused outside the door for a few seconds, their eyes locked in unmistakable lust.

"Damn, lad."

"Yeah. Let's unpack." Alex's eyes said *do me*. His body said *but not now*.

"The Americans have a word for it, naturally."

Alex cocked his head a little and grinned, mutely asking.

"Prick tease, Alex. Let's go inside and deal with the foogin luggage."

\*\*\*\*

Steve and his men had welcomed both of them to the dining table with warm handshakes and friendly smiles. Steve hadn't said a word about where they'd spent the night ... and Alex didn't bring it up. A brief spark in his eyes as he glanced at both of them was enough to convince Alex his host knew, and didn't care, that he and the Scotsman were already bedmates, or fast heading that direction.

Steve Long was a live-and-let-live kind of man, and Alex thought the people he surrounded himself with were probably the same. Unpretentious, smart, capable. After half an hour with them at the table, he felt as comfortable as he'd felt anywhere outside his own family, years ago, too many years back to allow easy memories to flow. He only knew this assignment was not a task but a godsend.

Once inside the cabin with Rory, he felt every tiny nerve begin to dance and quiver, starting and ending between his legs. Rory had not touched him with anything more tangible than his eyes, but that was enough to make his hands shake a little as he pulled the folded shirts from his suitcase and doubled them up on the meager supply of hangers. There was no dresser, and so he piled his socks and underwear on the seat of one of the wooden chairs. He slipped his Glock pistol under the socks. The sturdy Timberlands he was wearing would be his only boots on this trip—light enough for casual wear, durable enough for the roughest back country.

Rory had given up immediately. He'd packed so many changes of clothes there was no hope for more than a few shirts on the hangers, even though Alex had deliberately left most of them for his new friend.

"Crap, Alex. I'm a dolt. Why did I think I needed to dress like a bloody lord of the realm? All I need is a few shirts, a pair of ... you call them jeans? And maybe ... a pair of boots that don't pinch me all the way to the nuts."

Alex couldn't help it. Rory looked so disconsolate, like a kid whose cookie jar was on a shelf he couldn't reach, that he laughed, amused and aroused at the same time. In one step, Rory was pressed against the whole length of him, snugging Alex's crotch against his balls.

"Laugh at me, will you? Maybe my feet hurt, lad, but my cock is in fine fettle." He grasped him under the buttocks and raised him enough that both their zippers clashed, metal to metal, warriors pitted in battle. Rory managed to seize his lips, even though Alex was twisting his head in mock denial, and he began to nibble and suck as he talked.

"That bed is a bloody mockery. But fear not. Nothing can stop Rory Drummond—"

A sharp rap on the door froze both of them, and Alex found himself being the first to express his frustration. "Fuck." He slid down Rory and managed to stroke his cock back into a semblance of smooth.

Not bothering to tuck his shirt back in, he opened the door. It was Paul, the cook.

"Hi again, Alex. Steve wanted to know, as long as you were going into Ely, would you mind picking up some groceries at the Safeway's. I made a list..."

Alex smiled and took the paper from Paul, refusing the credit card the man he held out. "Don't worry about the money. We've got it. After all, both of us are more than a day early, right? Small price to pay for the great food."

Paul shook his head. "Don't piss off Steve. He won't like that."

Rory, who'd been fussing with the window, trying to stretch one of his large shirts across, joined them. "If someone could rig up a curtain, Paul, we'll call it more than even. I'm a shy kind of laddie, sad to say. Hate to give the visitors a glimpse of my blinding white haunches. Scare them before they ever see the snowdrifts. How about it?"

Paul looked from the window to Rory and back again, a slow smile spreading under the handlebar. "Sure, Rory. I gotcha covered." He winked and left them.

Rory looked as forlorn as before. "Hell. Now I don't know when he'll come pounding on the door again with a set of Queen Anne's lace draperies. We may as well leave."

He shrugged on a lined flannel jacket, and Alex zipped his own Gore-Tex. Standing close to the man who exuded the warmth of a fireplace, he put a hand on his forearm and smiled. "Maybe we can find a few minutes of privacy later. At least we'll be completely alone."

Rory bent a little and embraced him, enveloped his whole mouth, sucking his lips, then inserting his tongue. Releasing his mouth, he traced light hickeys up his cheek, into his ear. "I could foog you into tomorrow. Foog, laddie..."

Alex's greedy cock demanded he stand right there, returning his lover's wandering tongue. "Rory..."

Only the realization that Paul would no doubt come barging back any moment made Alex break away a little, and Rory didn't try to hold him. Alex imagined the skinny guy, all elbows and mustache, flying through the trees waving lace curtains. He laughed all the way to the van, while Rory scowled, trying to tame the lump in his Levi's, goose stepping presumably to relieve the pressure on his testicles ... or smarting from the blisters on his feet.

He was still smiling a little as he pulled onto the wide driveway and left the ranch, thinking about getting fooged into tomorrow. *Yes, goddamn it, Rory, I want you just as much, Lord have mercy on my aching balls.*

Rory was silent for a while, no doubt nursing his own private pain. When he turned the van onto Highway 50, heading northwest for Ely, his companion finally spoke.

"I did a little homework, Alex, believe it or not. Someone called this 'The Loneliest Road in America.' To me, it will always be the Highway to Heaven."

Alex let his right hand rest lightly on his companion's denim thigh. "I'll try to remember that. It's been a kind of sad road for me."

"Because of your early life, Alex?"

He thought about it a minute. "Not because of what happened out here on the mountain. Being with my dad was probably the happiest time of my life, until ... well, until now." Rory's huge hand covered his. "The reason is after he died, I couldn't bring myself to come here again. I thought every mile would tear a new gash in my gut. But hell..." He glanced at Rory's marvelous face, inclined toward him with a look of profound understanding. "Hell, Rory, now I want to go there, where *mi padre* showed me how to hunt. Delight you with the bristlecones, be the first to introduce you to the golden aspens, the limber pine..."

"Soon. I'll be meeting him soon."

"The pine?"

"*No, mi caro. Tu padre.*"

How did the man even guess at what his deepest heart kept telling him? Going back to Moriah was going back to Ramón Dominguez, back to the man he had desperately loved all his life. Steve had been right about one thing. He'd always felt a fierce need to protect his father, even though the elder Dominguez was a large, stern man who never quailed in the face of anything. He still felt that sense of protection, as though to let strangers stumble into their old hunting grounds was a kind of trespassing, a violation of trust.

But Rory was different. Already he figured the man could walk on snow like a deer, could sense the slightest shift in wind, would track any path to get to his destination. He didn't have to witness it. Something about him, and the way he was speaking volumes right now with just a few words ... Alex knew going back was the right thing to do.

He answered Rory with the only three words he could muster without showing too much emotion.

"*Sí, caro mio.*"

*Yes, you are right. My darling man.*

# Chapter Eight
## Kingdom Come

They were approaching the strange little oasis he'd eyed on the way to the ranch this morning, a petrol station and eating establishment, standing as a traveler's last relief on the road into Ely before the road began to curve into Connors Pass. His stubborn cock told him he needed that same final release.

"Alex. Pull behind that ... general store? I need to take a piss."

His companion smiled and slowed, then banked in behind the quaint cluster of clapboard buildings and hand-made signs telling him this was "Major's Place."

He unclasped his seat belt. "We can go inside, you know. Drink some coffee, take a wiz."

Rory shook his head and clambered out of the van, coming around to the driver's side. He didn't bother to shield his cock from Alex's sight as he brought it out of the confining Levi's, pissing damned near five feet from him as he watched his lover watch his prick, fighting the erection as his urine dribbled and sputtered into the dry ground.

Finally he could fight it no more. His prick had decided to stand sentinel out here in the fragrant brush, defying the cold wind, the distant hum of passing vehicles, and every effort Rory made to empty his bladder. Alex was too close, his own desire too adamant. He opened the passenger door, his Levi's gaping open and his cock stiff as a brick.

"You promised me a moment of privacy, laddie. I claim that moment for my own. Right now." He reached to Alex, sliding an arm behind the small of his back. His other hand took the man's denim crotch, his fingers in the crack and his thumb stroking the balls, easily bringing him from behind the wheel and into his chest.

The crotch was rock-hard, the chest was already heaving against his own as though in automatic denial. Alex pushed against his ribcage, his deep-set eyes defying this impetuous choice of love nest.

"Not here, damn it. Any freaking tourist could wander back here—"

"Don't fight me, lad. This is more private than our damn cabin. I want you." He buried his mouth in Alex's jaw, biting and murmuring, reached his ear, fucked it wetly.

Alex was angry, he saw that immediately, and the anger was palpable enough to sing to his ready prick, fire his asshole a mile up his butt.

"You can't just grab me any goddamn time you feel like it. Get that straight. I'm not your 'ho. Understand?"

"Nay." He began to finger the foogin buttons on Alex's shirt, not even smarting when he slapped his hands away with a resounding *smack*. "Do that on my ass, lad, and I'll come a mile high. God, yes, take down my trousers and show me how much you hate this."

Alex was a strong man, almost as powerful as his determined assailant. Rory knew he had the advantage, because the place between his lover's legs was so full of rock-hard cock the zipper had begun to gape open. No man so aroused would fight him until the bitter end. His desperate desire would overwhelm the instinct to fight back. He knew that fact intimately, and he used it.

He pinned Alex to the seat back and stared into the endless dark of his eyes. "Listen to me. The more you fight me, the more I want you. Want you to the foogin heart of me." Something flickered in the man's eyes, his tight mouth began to take on a loose, sulky pout. Instantly, Rory seized the advantage and began to bite the lower lip. He nibbled and gnashed, stroked and fondled until his lover's tongue began to answer. First hesitant, still unsure. Next seeking its own vengeance, almost choking him with stabs of powerful need, then tearing at his mouth until they were both drawing blood and moaning.

Rory managed to lower his Levi's to his thighs, then began to work on Alex's button. He was thrashing and struggling, and his knee connected with his chin, sending a sharp pain all the way to the top of his skull. He felt his own grin widen as the hard blow served to channel his lust into single-minded intensity.

"Fight me, lad. I swear to God I'll break your metal button. I'll tear the zipper from these bloody trousers."

Alex relaxed for a few heartbeats, breathing hard, enough time for Rory to pull the Levi's forcibly almost to his knees, exposing his sledgehammer of a cock.

"I want that up my ass."

"No."

"Show me how much you hate it, lad."

In a few deft moves, he was sitting on Alex's ramrod prick. He'd already palmed the gel from his Levi's pocket, and now he opened the cap with his teeth then spat it onto the seat. With one hand, he smeared lube over every finger and began to probe and withdraw until he saw Alex's eyes begin to glaze with the need for more, deeper.

"Show me how pissed you are. You prick."

He actually did not expect the stinging blow on his ass cheek which sent a crack of lightning into the farthest reaches of his ass. Now aroused fully as a maddened bull, desperate to encase that wedge of a wide cock, he grasped it, lubed it, and guided it straight up his butt.

"No!" Alex's cry came accompanied by another hard slap on the opposite cheek. His eyes watering at the intensity of his joy, Rory sank even deeper onto the blade of the man's weapon, needing to explode, yet still wanting his lover to blow his seed to kingdom come, all the way to his prostate and beyond, to the gates of heaven.

Letting Alex's thick cock coat his hole, he moved as a wave would seize the shore then recede, letting the instinctive rhythm intensify his lover's cries. When he saw the orgasm begin to build in the man's brooding eyes, he couldn't stop pushing the invading cock ever inward, the spasms of his entire asshole gripping the length of his lover's flesh while they screamed into each other's mouth, a primal roar of release.

Afterwards, he straddled Alex and smoothed his cheeks, traced his handsome jaw bristled with morning beard. Some instinct told him not to speak, to let the man come to terms with being almost bloody raped. His near gentleness now was a need as powerful as his earlier frenzy to seize and be seized. The calm after the storm. Two deep needs, each balancing the other.

"You are a bastard and a bully."

"Aye, lad."

"That's the last time you'll get the better of me."

Rory looked into his eyes, found a profound satisfaction there, and allowed himself a slight smile. "Good. I need to be taken down a few notches. You're the only man I've ever met who could do it."

Alex relaxed a little, allowing Rory's finger to continue its path along his jaw, down to the hollow of his throat.

"Do you think you have to make love like a bull elephant? Are you always so ... abrupt in your sex habits?"

"Sex habits? I have none. And until you lad, I've never made love to a man."

*Enough. Let me not get this close, else I may never pull away.*

He leaned a little and kissed Alex, as full of restrained passion as his torn lips would allow. "Time to find me a ten-gallon hat, Alex. All this riding has fired my need to be a cowboy."

When he saw his own smile returned, he eased off his lover's thighs and pulled his pants back up, found the lid of the gel and replaced it before putting it back in his pocket.

"Wait."

"Yes, lad?"

"What you said about making love... Never mind. I think maybe I'll figure it out for myself."

"When you do, Alex, tell me." He refused to look one more time into those eyes, pulling him to a place he'd never been before. Torn between fear and need, he relaxed again on the seat opposite the man who was driving him, all right ... driving him bloody crazy.

\*\*\*\*

All the way into Ely, Alex felt the effects of Rory's love making. Yes, love making. The man had admitted as much... As though their recent collision was more than raw need. He should have felt violated, the way Rory had seized him, had almost torn his

Levi's from his ass, forced his own over-wide cock up his big Scottish butt.

The thought of it made his prick stand and cheer again, even twenty minutes later as they were easing off the pass, the Sport Van consuming the last miles between heaven and Ely, Nevada.

He allowed his mind to linger at Major's Place. Five minutes after his cum had shot up Rory's asshole, he'd still been fighting it, all the while knowing it was the best sex he'd ever experienced. And then the man had gentled him with his luminous green eyes and the soft burr of his voice, his tender finger tracing his mouth

Christ, it had been a trip to paradise. He'd thrashed against it and denied it, his very resistance seeming to fire Rory's greed for him. He could understand the rough sex; even though it was new to him, he'd heard guys talking about it, had never understood the allure. What he couldn't understand was his own reaction, his screaming need to spank and slap his lover, releasing some new kind of goddamn hormones into his system, whatever it was that had made him do it once, then again.

*Fuck. It was so good...*

And Rory had loved every second. Goaded him, rode him, reviled him until he struck out blindly, wanting to punish him, and Rory getting off on the punishment. This was a kind of love-making he wanted to explore, even though he knew the tiny cabin and the flimsy tents they'd no doubt share wouldn't be big enough for their passion.

His gaze flicked to Rory, who'd also been silent the last half hour as if he too was thinking about their side trip. As usual, his head was on the seat back, eyes shut as if asleep.

His eyes snapped back to the road, concentrating on getting them to Warren's Western Wear in one piece.

Maybe he'd turn on the radio, treat his new buddy to a little country-western singing.

"Music?"

"Your voice? Aye, lad. Sing me something in Spanish. I love that perfect language, the tongue of poets and architects."

Alex was amused at the deliberate misunderstanding. "I didn't mean me. I meant the radio."

"And I meant you."

When he looked over, Rory's deep eyes were trained on him, speaking something he wanted to hear more, closer, forever.

His eyes back on the road again, he let his own natural tenor rise in the confines of the van, somehow not embarrassed because after all, it was the language of his fathers.

*Aquellos ojos verdes*
*de mirada serena,*
*dejaron en mi alma*
*eterna sed de amor.*

"More, Alejo."

A burning around his eyes made him squeeze them shut for an instant, fighting against the memory of his own father singing those same words, far older even than his own grandfather. Yet the words sang also to the present, to his growing need for this stranger next to him.

*Those green eyes ... their serene gaze ... they left in my soul ... an eternal thirst to love.*

"Um, maybe later, Rory. Serenades are for moonlight."

"And for lovers."

*Fuck. This man is far too much for me to handle. He probably knows every freaking word of the song, somehow... He can probably read my own thoughts.*

He glanced once more at Rory Drummond, indolently stretched alongside him, and he felt his heart stutter just a little. Just enough to know it was time to stop daydreaming. "We'll be there any minute, Rory. Like I said, later. Okay?"

"Okay, Alex. Tell me how you know *una canción cubana*. Is that your family's homeland?"

"Cuba? No, my grandfather emigrated here from Colombia. I'm third generation. Far enough from my heartland to remember the *empanadas* my mother used to make. That's about it."

"Colombia is a land of sheer beauty ... mountains that put even these to shame. The mighty Andes. Why did your grandfather leave?"

"My father said, he was trying to protect his family. From the endless guerilla fighting, the night attacks that left even children dead for no reason. The violence never reached the door of my grandfather. But then, he never gave it a chance."

After a while his curiosity got the better of him. "And you ... how is it you know Spanish? Know about my homeland? Even about Cuban songs?"

"Because, *mi caro*, I love the language. It is a tongue that naturally sings, from the heart of whole nations of people who delight me. Starting with the one alongside me."

The outskirts of Ely hove into view, and Alex was almost sorry to end their conversation, subtly on the edge of confession, full of veiled endearments. He sighed and smiled, not turning to look at his passenger.

*Tu me gusta también. You please me, too, Rory Drummond.*

The sales clerk at Warren's, Alex saw, was trying to hide a shit-eating grin as his companion tried on one badly-sized hat after another.

"What think you, lad? Is it me?"

He looked at a black hat, some brand he didn't know, one that hardly fit Rory's large head. It seemed to ride on top like a full-sized man on a pony.

"Um ... hold on." He fingered the selection of hats on a nearby shelf and handed his companion a soft Stetson of brown-red leather, almost the color of his luminous hair. "Try this one." Rory settled it down over his head and looked at him, making his prick jump six inches. It was freaking perfect. The combination of the color and the brim tipped over his sexy eyes made the man look like someone's wet dream of a cowboy.

"Will you believe me if I say 'perfect,' my friend? Because it is. Made for you."

Rory grinned. "And I believe you, lad. If you like it, that's the final word." He leveled his eyes at the clerk. "Don't bother to bag it, my fine man. I'll wear it out of the store. How much?"

Alex saw the clerk's eyes reach somewhere beyond Rory's large smile, down to his crotch then back up to the handsome face. Unaccountably, he felt a little jealous.

"For you ... Let's say two hundred dollars. Not a dime more."

As they were getting back in the van, Alex couldn't help pausing at the door, looking across at Rory. "Now I'll have to start wearing my gun, goddamn it, Drummond, to fight off the admirers. You're a natural."

Rory winked at him, then slid onto the seat and slammed the door. Before they took off for the grocery store, he rested his large hand for a moment on his thigh. "Whatever I have, it's yours. You know that."

Alex knew this was no time for subtle endearments. He had to keep his mind on business, at least until they returned to the ranch.

"Then I'd like your cowboy boots."

"Really?"

"Yes, really." He was convinced the boots were an abomination before the Lord, and someone needed to gently pry them from the Scotsman's death grip.

"Okay, Alex. But you'll have to help me pick out another pair."

Alex grinned. "It's a done deal. C'mon, let's go back and delight the sales clerk."

It took no more than half an hour, and when at last they emerged from the store, Rory was wearing a pair of honest-to-God leather boots, wide enough for his feet, with a heel that didn't threaten to topple the man whenever he took a step. And they were almost as handsome as he was, a soft brown leather with subtle tooled designs that said, "I'm too sexy for my boots, but I'm wearing 'em anyway."

This time before they got in the van, Rory thrust the bag at him, the one containing his alligator darlings.

"I want to see you wear these, lad. Just for me."

He looked deep into Rory's humor-filled eyes. "I will. I promise." On a night when he was naked and roaring drunk, some day before he left, he hoped he'd wear those boots just for Rory, the comical prelude to a damn good fuck.

# Chapter Nine
## To Make Love

When they passed Major's place once more, traveling back to the Long Trails Ranch, he extended his legs as far as he could, letting the rumble of the tires under his butt and the sight of a handsome, silent driver keep his mind on personal matters.

Rory was as happy as he'd ever been in his life. More, probably. He'd told Alex the bald truth ... that he'd never really made love to another man. He'd pounded many a hole with his insatiable cock. He'd rimmed puckered assholes and had his own hole licked, he'd sucked hard dick and had his own cock blown to smithereens. He'd spanked and whipped and had his own skin flayed, he'd bound others and been trussed himself like a foogin Christmas duck. He'd played every known sex game and had even made up a few of his own. But it was emphatically not making love. More like making lust, spilling seed, needing to empty himself of a physical urgency before turning to other matters.

As many times as he'd emptied, he'd not once found satisfaction beyond a few seconds of pent-up cum shooting or dribbling from his hungry prick.

*Is that any way to live, Rory, me lad?*

His unending search for sex partners was probably a reflection of some goddamn need to find the real thing. *Sodding goddamn fact, laddie ... you need a real man to fire your ass and tame it too. Capture and channel your wild prick. Someone like Alex.*

In a few years, he'd be thirty years of age. Well past the time he should decide what he wanted to be when he grew up. His father had controlled his own wanderlust, had found a woman who'd put up with his nonsense and who'd subtly shaped it to produce a son and a contented life. Kenneth Drummond, unlike his brother Robert, wanted none of the political life, or even the life of a country squire. He seemed happy to putter around Drummond Castle, lay in nine holes of golf, listen to Rory's travelogues, stroke Cathleen Drummond's hand by the stone fireplace while the winter wind battered the towers of the small castle he'd inherited and had already passed to his son.

When Rory left for more than a week, which sometimes happened, Kenneth Drummond picked up the laird responsibilities with Alan Cameron's help. If he did more than that, Rory wasn't home long enough to see it.

He absolutely did not want to live the passive life of a castle keeper. But by God and all the saints, he hated the life he'd been living, despised the man he'd let himself become. He wanted to welcome the future with a vengeance, claiming some grip on satisfaction. On happiness.

Last night in the motel... A few hours ago behind that rustic way-station... That was love making. That was a striving to give his partner something back, even if he himself had to give up an orgasm. That was a goddamn tenuous, delicate and altogether satisfying experience he had to call creating love. Love making.

"A crowned thistle, Rory. For your thoughts."

He roused himself at the sound of Alex's voice, teasing and warm.

"Thinking about my life, lad. Or the lack of it."

"You're unhappy?"

He deftly skirted the truth. He was happy now, at this miracle of a moment. But his real life waited in a lonely castle, far from these boundless skies, this endless valley. "Just the opposite, Alex. By God, I wouldn't trade this moment for any other."

Alex glanced over at him and offered his hand, which he took and lightly held, as though it was a gift of cobwebs and sea foam. "I ... ah, I feel the same."

His simple words filled the van like a melody. Rory sat with his heart hammering against his ribs, needing to say something, failing, just holding a little more tightly to Alex's offered prize.

Could this be the same Rory Drummond who'd boarded a plane in Edinburgh, Scotland? Because five minutes after touching down in a rustic air field in Nevada, he reckoned he was a changed man. Or could be, if somehow he could make this very moment into an eternity.

He clamped shut his mind, refusing to think past the present. His whole life, he'd not allowed sobriety to interfere with a good foogin drunk. And right now he was inebriated, pure and simple. Drunk on this man, this straightforward and honest man. *Alejo, Alejandro. Yo te quiero...*

"We have maybe half a day to ourselves, Rory, before we pick up the other fellows. What would you like to do tomorrow?"

"You want the truth? Park this big-butted van somewhere and love your ass into next week."

"Not an option. As they say, been there, done that."

Alex grinned and withdrew his hand to make the turn to the ranch, setting it back on the wheel as if that was the answer to his fanciful scenario.

"You want it. You crave it, lad. Be honest. Because I'm honest with you when I say I'll 'love your ass.' And every other part of you too. Even your sassy mouth. Maybe especially that." He reached over and drew his thumb along Alex's lower lip, letting his cock rejoice at the touch.

In answer, Alex seized his thumb with his teeth and bit down, just hard enough to send several watts of voltage up his asshole. Again.

"By God, Alex. That tiny cabin has no chance of staying in one piece. Tonight I'll tear it into kindling, I foogin promise..."

The road under his behind was bumpy enough to make Rory sit up straight in the seat and tuck his cock back into some semblance of law and order. He thought about Alex being a policeman and frowned slightly.

"Do you think you could enforce the law anywhere, lad? Nevada ... Texas ... Scotland?"

Alex laughed out loud. "That came out of freaking la-la land. What do you mean?"

He tried to keep his tone bantering, almost teasing. "Oh, just wondering how strongly your job holds you to this place."

"I think I could be a cop anywhere, Rory. But it's definitely something I like doing. I'd like it even better if I weren't by myself so goddamn much. The highways can be ... endless sometimes."

"Maybe there's a job that's not so lonely. Maybe even in an entirely different place..."

Alex glanced at him, one brow cocked. "Like where?"

"Bloody hell, laddie, how would I know? Just curious." *Careful, lad. Quicksand ahead.*

"I've done this almost four years now. Maybe soon I'll have enough experience under my belt to apply for a real cop's job. Or maybe a deputy sheriff position. I'm not pushing it, Rory. Let the chips fall, the old saying goes."

"All right, Alex. I just want ... I just want you to be happy."

"I am. Right now, I'd say I'm happier than I've been for more than ten years." Rory saw a smile tip a corner of his brooding mouth. "And tonight, we'll test the timbers on that goddamn cabin. Okay?"

They pulled into the drive, and Alex stopped the van near the ranch house front porch. "If you'll carry that box of groceries to the house, we can wash up, change, get ready for supper."

Rory muscled the large carton of supplies up the porch and before he could knock, the door opened. It was Steve Long, and he was scowling.

"Hey. I'm a little pissed you wouldn't let me get these groceries. So you'll have to eat extra to make up for it."

"Don't say that, lad. You'll be a poor man for letting me."

"Supper's at six. You're late, you eat leftovers. Got it?"

Rory was catching on quickly to the little phrases everyone around him used, mostly to ask for a thumb's up.

"Um, got it." He passed the box to his host. "See you then, Steve."

"Oh ... and Rory?"

"Yes?"

"Nice fucking hat."

Rory grinned and touched the brim, just as he'd seen cowboys do in a few TV westerns. He walked back to join his lover, smiling into the dark eyes in the driver's seat watching his every move. When he got back in the van, he leaned toward him and breathed in his ear, teasing a little about the future state of their cabin. "Kindling wood, lad. Small enough pieces to feed a bloody campfire. I promise."

\*\*\*\*

Alex spent almost the whole trip back from Ely thinking about his companion. A man of huge sexual appetite, yet also one of intelligence, compassion, humor... It would be hard to name a virtue he did not have. Except maybe restraint.

He wondered how many men Rory had taken, in whatever form that word implied. Taken, seduced, fucked, sucked ... loved.

And yet he'd told him, straightforward as hell, that Alex was the first man he'd ever made love to. That was the puzzle he'd spent most of today trying to explain to himself. For sure, Rory had pounded his share of men. He made no bones about his gayness, he was sure of himself in bed.

*Last night in the motel, he let me capture him, like a horse letting a cowboy slip a halter over his head, knowing he could escape with a mere toss of his mane. He allowed it, he wanted it, he gave me that chance to show my own horny need. And he goaded me into slapping his ass in the van this morning, knowing I'd love it too. Guiding me, teaching me.*

He wanted to say, *loving me* ... but the idea was too new, too impossible, to look at squarely. He tucked it away somewhere to bring out later, maybe in the dark of night, alone with his private demons, denying such a miracle could happen to him.

Looking over at Rory had become a favorite pastime, and he did it again. The Scotsman was stretched out, his hat tipped over his eyes, his feet in his new boots crossed, looking wholly relaxed. The sight of the gorgeous cowboy and his hefty crotch made his lips twitch in humor ... and yes, lust too. He felt his damned Levi's getting tighter by the moment.

So why did his relative back in Scotland need someone to keep an eye on him? It made no damn sense. He drank, yes, but he was large enough and smart enough to handle it well. He was an experienced deerstalker. He was practiced in the social arts. Rory had a quiet competence that gave the lie to Alex's stupid assignment. Hell, Rory in a way was watching over him, keeping him from falling into despondency, from brooding about his early life and his dead-end job.

*Face it. Rory is making me happy as a giddy adolescent. Hell, I've never felt so alive, so full of cockiness and cum. Then why am I letting this charade continue? Why don't I tell Rory the truth and be done with it?*

He knew why, even as he mulled the question over and over. Because he'd been handed an assignment to complete. And he was a good cop. He obeyed orders. The fact that this particular order seemed stupid should not matter. He'd already broken the spirit of the law when he gave his willing body to Rory.

However ... the assignment might even lead to a promotion. The governor was depending on him. But who was more important—the governor of Nevada ... or Rory Drummond? A man cattle-prodded by political interests to handing out an ill-advised order? Or his worldly and caring and altogether fascinating lover?

He tried his best to let the difficult questions slide to the back of his mind, where he could deal with them later. If he didn't think much about it, maybe the problem would somehow solve itself. *Seguro, Alejo. Close your eyes and the boogeyman will just go away.*

In spite of their good-natured bantering and brief hand-holding—or maybe because of it—Alex began to feel the first sharp talons of regret at his own dishonesty start to curl into his gut, draw blood, then lodge there.

He dug in his watch pocket and produced the door key while Rory waited next to him. When he opened the door and they both walked in, neither of them waited five seconds even to take a wiz. No sooner had he drawn the latch over the door than he felt Rory's unmistakable fist-hard signal in the small of his back, his long arms wrapped around him, the soft beard brushing his ear. "Alejo."

He turned his head, trying to move in his lover's greedy hold. "Oh, God, Rory, I—" His lips were stilled with a mouth that whispered and nibbled, sucked and sampled and thrust fire down his throat. Both of them lapping and spitting and biting, they kissed for long minutes, until finally Rory let him go.

"Foog, lad. I need to take a piss. Do not move."

For the first time since entering, he looked around at the tiny room. Instead of two spindly cots, he saw one oversized bed pushed to the wall, covered with a quilt. Conscious that there was only feeble light in the place, he saw the window was covered with what seemed to be a chenille bedspread, like one he had on his own bed as a child. As Rory would say, a foogin Queen Anne's lace curtain, by God, promising all the privacy they could ask for.

He also saw their host had provided a table, large enough to hold a Coleman lantern with space to lay a few other articles if they needed to. Better than the Waldorf Fucking Astoria. He laughed out loud.

Rory emerged from the can, looking around with a puzzled frown.

"I think Steve Long has our number, Rory."

Rory grinned and walked to him, smoothing his hair back a little with his large hand, pushing a strand behind his ear. "Aye. That number is one, lad. You plus myself equals one."

"Did Steve tell you when supper would be served?"

"Six o'clock. We have almost a whole hour."

He stood close to Rory, letting him crush his chest into his wide ribcage, loving the feel of his crotch rubbing against a wide expanse of very hard denim. "You are a freaking liar, my friend. We have less than half an hour."

Alex pulled back and studied the man's handsome face, admiring the clouds of red-gold hair in the light coming through the pale yellow chenille spread. "How did I deserve you? You've changed me from a prick to a prince."

His lover laughed, a sound of delight that warmed him to the core. "Prick. Aye, I called you a prick today, lad. And so you were. And now, if you'll make love to me, you'll change into a handsome prince. Will you?"

"Make ... love ... to you? Yes. I'd like that, Rory. Never tried to ... to do that before. Give me time to get it right, would you?"

The man in the cowboy hat and boots, wearing his tight jeans with more swag than a movie star, cupped his face in his enormous hands. "I get it, Alex. You just need me to back off a little. I can do that. I'll give you all the time you need, lad. I'll give you anything in the world."

Alex let him draw his mouth softly to his own, felt the tender beginnings of a shy kiss, answered with a longing he thought he'd buried more than a decade ago ... the need of a man for love, for solace, for understanding.

*Te quiero.* He mouthed the words against Rory's soft lips and did his best to still the rampant beating in his chest he was sure the other man could hear and translate, as surely as he'd understood his earlier love song to those remarkable green eyes.

*Love at first sight. Why the hell not?*

# Chapter Ten
## Novice Dom

Supper was another convivial gathering, this time with seven additional men who rubbed elbows—literally—as everyone ate together at the long cedar table. Alex reckoned this was Steve's entire crew. Wranglers, ranch workers, large animal handlers, men who put in a hard day's work for the reward of a hard life in this thirsty valley. He wondered what would keep a fellow out here, putting up with the soul-sucking heat of Nevada's summers and her bitch-slap of freeze in the winter.

*Maybe they thrive on the harshness. On the eternal promise of the mountains to provide snow for the groundwater. And on each other.*

His eyes naturally traveled to the man seated next to him. *Now I have someone too. For a split second in time, I have someone to call my own.* The sweetness of having Rory and the bitter thought of its fleeting joy made him sink his head for a few seconds to his plate, hoping no one had caught his tell-tale rapid blinks, trying to stop the burning behind his eyes.

When he glanced back up, Rory was looking at him, a world of affection reflected in the still pool of his eyes. Under the table, Alex briefly laid his hand on the Scotsman's denim-clad knee, squeezed it a little, then rested his arm again on the table top.

After supper, cold as it was outside, half of them sat on the porch while the rest drifted into the darkness beyond the gas lantern hanging from a hook, illuminating faces rough with stubble. Someone began to blow a mouth harp. He let the bluesy riffs echo off his memory and again settled into the comfort of knowing Rory was close beside him. He was deaf to the murmured conversations around him, thinking about his promise to the big man. To make love. To find somewhere in his limited experience the knowledge of how to create a unique pleasure for a man who'd felt it a thousand times over.

The wail of the harmonica, the sudden burst of Rory's laughter at some wry comment, the puffs of condensation as all of them breathed out the crisp night air ... all of it began to set up a rhythm in his mind, and he relaxed into the knowledge he could do about anything to Rory and the man would lie and say he loved it.

After a while, Steve rose from an old rocker. "My bed time, boys. You all have a good night. See you at breakfast." Before he opened the door, he turned and leveled his eyes at Alex. "Four guests are arriving at the airport tomorrow, Jack tells me around noon. Will you and Rory handle that for me?"

"A pleasure, Steve."

He smiled. "If anyone's hungry, ask 'em to have a bite of lunch there near the airport. I'll have a welcoming buffet later on, around four. Happy cat-herding." He shut the door behind him.

He smiled at Rory and mouthed, "Ready?"

Without answering, Rory stood, eclipsing everyone around him. "Let's try to find our way in the dark, lad. You're my buddy. So if I fall, you'll have to catch me."

Alex grinned and nodded to the men on the porch, then followed a large figure who was all too rapidly becoming part of the shadows. Rory had no idea at the length of his own strides.

"Hey, buddy."

The figure stopped.

"I have your back. You need to have mine. So slow your roll, okay?"

When he joined Rory, their fingers naturally twined in the welcome darkness, and somehow they made their way to what had already become the most important place in the world ... their flimsy, cold, too-small, altogether private heaven of a cabin.

Alex turned on the Coleman, then the space heater. They hadn't wanted to risk leaving it on while they were gone. No sense burning down the ramshackle place before they'd even slept a night in there.

Rory emerged from the euphemistic bathroom and sat on the edge of the new bed.

Alex still couldn't believe their fortune. "How the hell did they get that bed in here?"

"Because, lad, it's two doubles pushed together. So be careful ... don't fall in the crack."

Alex couldn't help it. He leaned down to his companion and brushed his ear with his tongue, then murmured a few words. "Only one crack I'll fall into. Be careful yourself." Rory lifted his head to start a kiss, and Alex deliberately avoided contact. "Nuh-uh. My turn. You'll do as I say."

When Rory sat back balanced on the heels of his hands and grinned, Alex reached over and removed the cowboy hat.

"We'll start right here, hombre." He removed it and tossed it to the top of his pile of socks on the chair. Running his fingers through the man's cornsilk hair, he brought them around slowly to burrow in the soft hair of his short beard; and leaning forward, he ran his tongue from Rory's inner ear, across his cheek, to his upper lip.

Speaking into his mouth, he rasped, "You'll start with giving me your feet so I can undress you."

He felt himself shaking, his gut playing games with the muscles in his thighs and calves. But Rory was silent, following his orders. *I can do this. I can try to act out every sex fantasy I've ever had, and make up new ones as I go along.*

He squatted at the side of the bed while Rory lifted one foot. He grasped the heel of the boot and eased it off, sliding it over the arch, thumbing the meat under the big toe a little as he lowered the foot to the rough boards on the floor. Then he removed the other boot, letting it fall with a decisive thump.

With both bare feet in front of him, he knelt, resting them on his knees. He began to stroke them at the same time, allowing his fingers and thumbs to trace circles and infinities—hard—into the flesh under his toes, then on the sole, the heel, and back up to the toes. His efforts were rewarded with a low moan. "God, lad. Keep it up and I'll come in my jeans."

"Quiet." He put Rory's left big toe in his mouth and began to lick, then suck, all the while his hands played at loving the man's skin while Rory crooned his delight. The toe might as well have been the man's hefty cock, the way he suckled and slavered, pretending, creating fairy tales on the sensitive flesh.

Alex glanced up. Rory was lying back on the bed, his chest rising and falling as though he'd been running a hard race... The huge mound in his Levi's was moving, and Alex took pity on the groin while deliberately abandoning both quivering big toes. Standing up and leaning a little, he deftly slid the metal button free of the denim, then pulled the zipper, freeing the cock to stand and crow.

*Fuck.* This man's pride was what a Greek god would wear, if Greek gods still roamed the earth. Perfect, long and wide, the pronounced ridge making it look like the hilt of a weapon. *This battle ax was up my ass.* The thought of it made his entire groin and the depths of his butt throb in expectation.

He continued the gruff orders. "Lift your butt a little." Then, "Don't fight me, goddamn it. Let me slide them over your legs." When the Levi's were a heap on the floor, he began to work the shirt buttons free of their holes, slowly, watching Rory's prick dance to the rhythm of his fingers.

All at once, Alex saw himself not as a sex-deprived man living out a fantasy. He was the Velvet Lover, the one to free his lover's cum from his dick, by whatever path he deemed necessary ... slow, ball-tightening and excruciating in its intensity.

He peeled the flannel shirt back from Rory's shoulders, exposing the muscled breasts and pronounced nipples. Alex knelt on the bed between his lover's splayed knees and grazed, pulling the nipples with his teeth, sucking each in turn, imagining his lover's ass muscles contracting as he prayed and played at the shrine of Rory Drummond.

"Alejo, let me foog you."

He looked up into a storm at sea, Rory's entire face convulsed with something between pain and joyful abandon.

He forced a gravelly, harsh tone into his voice. "Wait."

He stood and took off his own boots. Quickly unzipping his Levi's, he let them puddle at his feet, then stepped clear. His shirt followed, falling in a heap on the abandoned denims.

He climbed back between Rory's tree-trunk thighs, letting his balls trail across the man's fist-tight scrotum. Extending forward, he kissed his lover on the mouth, then crawled back down to his groin. He scooped the cock into his mouth as far as he could, reveling in the musky tang of the flesh and the ropiness of trellised veins.

"Do it, lad, suck me dry."

He let the cock drop from his mouth as he knelt over Rory's tangled mass of pubic hair, licking the length of it nested there, extended almost to the navel.

He spoke as he tongued Rory's entire groin ... the bulb of the cock, the thick shaft, the swollen balls. "Goddamn it, man, I said to be quiet. Can't you follow a simple—" The *thwacck* on his ass spilled a pool of cum from his slit, tore through his asshole, all the way up somewhere into his belly.

"Trying to play the tough guy, Rory? You'll fucking lie there and do whatever I tell you. Got it?"

With a bellow, Rory sat up, lifting Alex's ass off his thighs and applying his flat palm again, a slap that jarred his back molars and made him almost come right there on his lover's balls.

"Make me be quiet, Alex. Foogin make me."

"Bastard! Lie back! Lift your legs. Or else..."

Rory was panting. "Or else what?"

Alex grinned, the smarting of his ass chasing itself up his shaft and out the slit. He was dribbling again, close to coming. "Or else I'll never be able to stuff my prick up your ass. Do what I say."

When Rory lay back again and lifted his legs, Alex remembered the lube, somewhere in the man's Levi's. He quickly found the jeans, palmed the gel and gave the tube to Rory. "When I'm through sucking your asshole, spread this on my cock. Will you?"

Without waiting for an answer, kneeling between Rory's legs, he bent and lifted the massive balls, spread his thighs, and thumbed his cheeks wide. He found the puckered hole. This was something he'd never done before, had fantasized about a hundred times while masturbating. Letting his inhibitions float away, he inserted his tongue and began to thrust it wetly, then out again, his cock stiff enough to hammer nails.

"Do you ... love it ... Rory?" He spoke slow, in between the frenzied proddings of his tongue.

"God, Alex, never stop. Tongue-fuck my asshole..."

He licked and slavered and sucked until he felt the cum rise in his balls. Lifting his head, he managed to groan, "Lube me. All over, quick."

His lover's hands were already thick with the stuff, and he slathered it onto his straining cock. With Rory's legs on his shoulders, Alex rammed his greased flesh into Rory's soaking-wet hole before his cock could detonate.

Here was an experience he would carry with him the rest of his life. His cock buried up Rory's butt, his lover's head back, his mouth open as he rammed and withdrew, thrust and pulled almost all the way out. The walls of hot muscle were caving in on his prick, begging him to fuck harder, deeper.

He put his tongue in Rory's open mouth and fucked it, too, loving him, needing him, still waiting for his lover to feel the ecstasy. His fingers found the nipples and pulled in rhythm with his instinctive thrusts.

The words were brief, and so full of anguished desire he began to shoot his cum to the full extent of his long cock. "Now. Alejo, now."

He felt the cave walls vibrate all along his prick even while it erupted into a molten, moving cavern. The release seemed to last long minutes while he burrowed harder, deeper into his lover's heat.

He collapsed on Rory's chest, letting him stroke his back and suck his mouth. "*Caro mio*, Alejo, I loved that."

Alex's face was buried in his throat. He managed to lift his head a little, still hardly able to breathe. "You'd say that no matter what."

"Maybe. I have no way of knowing. Because I foogin loved it."

They lay together, locked in an embrace, while the night stole its full measure of blessed oblivion.

\*\*\*\*

Rory woke once, wondering where he was. When he saw the tangles of dark hair on his chest and felt Alex's strong arms around him, he closed his eyes and smiled.

There was no doubt in his mind. Alex was ready for the next step. It wouldn't be long before he had the man tying him, blindfolding him, playing dom to his willing sub. And then he'd show Alex how it was really done. Two strong men trying to subdue each other, loving the battle, succumbing when the time was right.

He knew it was not the classic dom-sub psychology, and he didn't care. In fact, he reveled in the expression of his own unique vision of love. A tussle, a give and take, a pitched battle that ended with both of them ejaculating into forever.

He lowered his head a little and kissed the damp hair.

*Alejo. My dom. The man who made love to me.*

The thought of it stirred his sleeping cock. *Yes, he made love. To me. And I loved him back. Sweet Mary and all the bloody prophets, this man was performing an act of love.*

He began to count their days remaining together. Tomorrow, the meeting of the hunters. Next day, no doubt the first short group excursion, getting to the base camp, feeling out the environment, getting used to the rifles and equipment. Third day, maybe their first hike past the sheltering camp, letting their legs limber and their lungs get used to the thinner air.

And then ... it might be four, five days, before Steve decided his big game hunt had been successful and began to lead his charges off the mountain. So he and Alex had less than a week to be together.

And then what? He tightened his arms around the man in his arms and once more kissed his rumpled hair. And then he'd have to decide, for once and for all, whether he'd finally grow up and take his man fully, in every sense of the word.

And would this marvelous man accept him? He didn't want to ... he couldn't ... confront the possibility that Alex would turn away. *He made love to me. I could tell it was honest and pure. Damn it, Alejo, stay with me.*

When he slept again, it was a fitful slumber. But he would not toss and turn, for fear he'd wake Alex.

*My dom worked hard for me tonight. Let him sleep.*

# Chapter Eleven
## Herding Cats, Taking Baths

**R**ory waited with Alex at the same Gate Two where he'd tottered down the ramp to his new freedom. The ranch guests were easy to spot. All coming from the same connecting flight out of Houston, they walked together, laughing and talking easily among themselves, already friends.

Rory saw immediately that one man, a little shorter than the others and maybe a shade older than Steve, walked with a certain assurance and a roll to his shoulders that marked him right away as an outdoorsman. He himself had been on many a deerstalking; and that man had the unmistakable look of one who'd know what he was doing on a big game hunt.

Rory estimated his height at about five feet ten inches, and his weight perhaps two hundred. A little heavy for his height, but it was mostly in his chest and not his gut. He was chatting with a man a little taller and slight of build, one in his late forties or early fifties. He was thin of leg, thin of hair, and Rory guessed he was probably built like a trolley rail. It was hard to tell, dressed as he was in a parka the envy of any Eskimo. Rory immediately pegged him as a novice, one who might spend more time at a campfire than on a trail. Yet he seemed to be a man of humor, throwing back his head and laughing at something his companion had said, a man with smile crinkles at the side of his pale brown eyes.

Almost abreast with those two, a third man listened and smiled as he walked. This one was youngish—maybe thirty-five—with straight brown hair and untidy bangs that hung in his eyes. Serene of face, almost casual in his stride, his eyes were taking in every detail of the small de-boarding area. He walked with partly sloping shoulders, hands in pockets, and even from almost thirty feet he seemed to make eye contact. Nodding a little, a slight smile hooking his mouth, he continued sauntering with his companions while Rory eyed the fourth man taking up the rear all by himself.

A grizzly bear of a man, he wore a beard standing out from his cheeks by a few inches, much longer than Rory's closely shaped one. He was the tallest of his mates, almost the height of Alex, with burly shoulders and heavy brows. Wearing only an open flannel jacket, Rory was impressed already with the large man's movements, far more nimble than a man his size should be.

"Rory, let's meet them before they decide to split up and lose us."

"You mean go down the drain in the privy like I did, lad?"

Alex waggled his eyebrows "Exactly."

Both laughing, they moved to intercept the four passengers just moving past the roped-off area at the end the ramp.

Rory held up his hand, a giant of a signpost. "Anyone looking for Long Trails Ranch?"

"Yo."

The man he'd eyed first spoke up and motioned to his companions to stop. They mutely followed him to an open space near the seating area.

*Natural leader. I like that.*

He held out a hand to the one he'd tabbed as head of the group, and the man immediately seized it. "Mark Sumner. Glad to meetcha. This here..." he looked at Eskimo Man, "...this is Ralph Gore."

Ralph grinned and pumped his hand, then Alex's. "Ralph Gore, the guy with more. Can you tell I'm a salesman?"

Alex was grinning, a mischievous look in his eye. "Um, kinda."

"I'm Drew." The youngest of the four, the one with a high forehead and straight brown hair, stepped to shake Rory's hand, then Alex's. He turned to the grizzly. "Sam...?"

"Sam Wakefield, out of Corpus. Happy to meet you fellas." Rory gripped the paw of the bear, enjoying the challenge of a grip almost as forceful as his own.

Rory noticed immediately the one called Drew seemed to defer subtly to Sam; and that the skinny Ralph looked to Mark. Natural pairing. That would make their host's job of sorting "hunt buddies" fairly easy.

Alex cleared his throat. "Gentlemen. I'm Alex, and this is Rory. We're here a mite early, so our host wanted us to be the welcoming committee. But we're all in this together. Um, all for one..." He grinned and stopped talking. Rory had a feeling Alex was not the sort to make a speech.

In a rush of back-patting and chuckles, the six men stood for a while in a knot, deciding who needed to wander to the privy, how soon they needed to claim their luggage, and who among them were hungry enough to stop for food before they left for the ranch.

"Meet right here in exactly fifteen minutes..." But Rory was speaking to their backs as the four men paired off and drifted away.

Alex winked. "Herding cats."

"Aye, lad. An apt phrase. Mark Twain?"

Alex met his eyes. "Could be. I don't care, amigo. As long as I don't lose you again in this goddamn place."

He laid his hand a moment on his lover's arm. *You'll lose me, lad, when hell has igloos.* "No, nay, never, no more. As the old song goes. Let's wait by the ramp entrance, Alex. Four grown men should find their own peckers, their own luggage, and the blokes who'll herd them somewhere or other to fill their bellies."

He idly read the electronic signs announcing arrivals and departures. He wondered briefly why none of them were to or from Alex's town of Elko; and then his thoughts were filled by the sight of the man's hot eyes trained on him with a look that clearly said, *I want you.*

By the time they rolled up the drive to Steve's rambling house in the eight-passenger van, they really had begun to talk and act like old friends.

He discovered the one called Mark Sumner, the one he'd pegged as an experienced hunter, really was. He lived somewhere in the East... New Hampshire, maybe ... in mountains that were honestly tall hills, and he tried to find a new place "out west" to hunt large game once a year.

He was shrewd and careful in his speech, habits Rory appreciated in any man. He'd be able to talk with Mark, trade tall tales.

The salesman Ralph Gore was what Alex called "a kick in the pants." He had a jest for almost any topic and a way of moving nervously that Rory found exhausting. *Maybe he'll not sit at a fire after all. More like pace around and try to sell his company's brand of life insurance to the foogin jackrabbits.* Still, he was jovial and open, someone who would absolutely be a man of his word. He liked Gore, who admittedly had never hunted anything bigger than a pheasant.

Drew something-or-other was rather a puzzle. He told Rory he had hunted off and on, a few times mule deer in Montana; but mostly he enjoyed hitchhiking through the U.S. looking for "experience." He was a frustrated writer, but none of them could get him to say what he wrote about other than "real life." Even as they drove, his sharp eyes took in every scene along the road, and he constantly jotted into a small notebook he fished out of his shirt pocket. He even snapped pictures through the window with a small digital camera he kept in a jacket flap.

"Well, lad, I hope you won't find life biting you in the butt in a snowdrift, halfway up the mountain. No time for book writing when reality's freezing your bollocks off."

Even Drew had joined everyone's laughter at that observation. "Yeah. As they say, Rory, 'reality bites.' I'll try to remember that."

From that moment on, Drew seemed to lean subtly toward him from his position in the seat just behind his own, ask his opinion endlessly, smile constantly, until Rory wished he'd go back to his notebook. He noticed Alex seemed a little annoyed at the attention this new man was giving him, glancing over with a slight frown when Drew began to ask him about his reaction to being in the U.S. Was Alex jealous? Rory decided that was not possible, but he could hope.

Sam Wakefield, Rory found, was as Texan as his size. He told everyone he lived presently in Corpus Christi. He'd been all through that huge state on different kinds of hunts, but this year his wife had nagged him into trying something new. He'd often wanted to visit Nevada, and he'd found the Long Trails Ranch in a web search.

Rory chuckled to find he'd read the same brochure, reproduced on the net, promising a taste of "rustic cabins" and "raw wilderness."

"Rustic they are, lad, and raw. With beds to match."

When they arrived, Alex pulled up in front of the house.

"Let's wait on the luggage. I'll pull in close to the cabin area after everyone gets out, and later on I'm sure one of Steve's men will show you where you'll be staying. So you can pull your bags out close to home, kind of. Okay?"

Everyone piled out except Rory, who settled back and eyed the driver.

"Get me to a raw cabin, lad. We'll let Steve sort out those cats from now on. While you and I test our rustic bed."

Alex drew his mouth into that sexy curl and let his eyes rest a second on the front of his Levi's. "One hour 'til the buffet, Rory."

"No. Buffet now. 'Tis you I need to eat." He tipped his new hat down over his eyes a little and cocked an eyebrow, allowing Alex to snap the brim askew with a tease of his fingers.

"No talking dirty, cowboy. We need to behave ourselves. Okay?"

"Try me, Alejo. I promise to be ... good. Very good."

They were still grinning at each other like adolescents when they reached the door of the only curtained cabin on the Long Trails Ranch.

\*\*\*\*

Alex stripped and entered the tiny bathroom while Rory was standing at the toilet, hardly more than a cast iron bowl with a flusher.

"Back off, lad. D'you want me to piss on the ceiling?"

Alex grinned as he rubbed his balls along Rory's naked bum trying to get around him, then stood regarding the grand bath, no more than a washtub on legs. "We have cold water to stand in, Rory, while we do a PTA."

"I am loath to ask."

"Pricks, tits, and armpits."

"Now?"

"Now."

He leaned into the metal contraption fitted with just one faucet and a plug. He put the stopper in the drain and turned on the water. Letting the cold water run, he managed to turn in the small space and began to unbutton Rory's shirt from behind while his lover was still trying to empty his bladder, somehow, with Alex's fingers on his nipples.

"I have ways of wreaking vengeance, lad."

"You'll thank me later." He continued halfway unbuttoning and halfway tweaking his lover's rock-hard nipples, until Rory turned and snagged his lower lip with his teeth, letting his Levi's fall to his knees.

"Goddamn you, Alex..." Rory drew him to his chest, biting until Alex tasted blood, savoring the coppery taste, already rigid as a rod in spite of the chill in the room.

Climbing into the tub, he challenged the other man. "Get naked."

"Too foogin cold, lad."

Why did he feel a sudden boldness, a looseness of tongue, with this sexy man? "Rory. When I kiss your ass, I want a fresh pucker in return. And you'll get the same from me. Okay?" He turned his face a little, feeling the flush in his cheeks, yet determined to say even more later, in bed. Rubbing soap on his cock, slicking it up to his asshole and over his balls, he continued upward to his chest, under his arms, back to his groin. When he was thoroughly lathered, he bent and ran a small washcloth through the running water, wincing as he let the ice cold water hit all the soaped places. Then he bent again and removed the stopper.

He climbed back out with shriveled balls and small drooping cock and eyed Rory, bare-ass naked, standing with his arms crossed over his huge chest, legs apart, his giant cock rearing from its tangle of red curls.

"Your turn to lose that swag, highlander. Get in."

"The reward is too much to pass by, Alejo." His companion moved his mouth in altogether a devilish twist and repeated Alex's moves: run the water, stand in tub, soap up and rinse off.

Alex stood at the doorway rubbing down with a thin towel, letting the space heater warm his flesh and the sight of Rory Drummond warm him from the inside out. The man hadn't lost a trace of his erection, even in the balls-numbing cold of the water.

He stood with rivers of water streaming down his muscled chest, through the hairs of his groin and legs, back into the washtub.

"Tell me, Alex. What is 'swag'?"

"What you have in spades, Rory. Come here."

Never feeling more aroused, more sure of his need, he ran the towel over the Scotsman's girth, led him to the side of the bed, and ordered him to stand there with his legs apart. Then he squatted and began to eat his shapely butt, slow and thorough. From the cheeks, his tongue slid down the crack to the glory hole.

"*Madre de Diós*, I want you. Bend a little more."

He grasped the cheeks, thumbed them apart and began to burrow his tongue into the tiny hole, feeling it open to his slow, wet jabs. Rory's entire ass was shaking, and he was moaning. "No. No. No. Foogin yes, lad, suck my asshole."

Slavering and sucking, listening to his lover's appreciative groans, Alex felt his cum weeping from the slit, needing to find release.

"Take me. I can't wait another fucking second."

Rory picked him up bodily and put him face-down on the bed, then climbed on until he was straddling his ass. "I want to eat yours too, lad."

"I'll come in five seconds flat."

"Then come."

Alex felt the tongue begin to lap, the slobbering of spit pooling in his asshole. He strained to lift his ass, open himself fully, while Rory thumbed his butt apart and inserted his long tongue.

"Stop it. Stop it, Rory. Just fuck me, let me have your prick."

"Beg me."

"Just fucking do it." He buried his face in the bed, steeling himself for the invasion. When it began, when he felt the prick slide in past his rectal muscle, he almost bucked Rory off in his sudden pain and sweet, deep pleasure.

"Beg me, I said."

The hot probe gave way to a sudden emptiness, and Alex longed to be filled completely, forever. "Please. Please. Please. Pl—"

His asshole had become a mass of quivering flesh, pumping of its own accord, while Rory pushed his molten cock to the farthest haven he could provide. He began to come in unending shudders of joy, crying into the bed, loving the man who pounded him into a state of ache and ecstasy.

After a while, Rory eased off his back and lay next to him, his strong arms pulling him close again. "That was the appetizer, lad. Damn, you are a prick full." He sought his lips, seeming to take care to be gentle this time. They lay close until Alex was afraid they might miss Steve's welcoming remarks. They rose from the bed and dressed by touch, never taking their eyes from each other.

He wondered what his lover was thinking as his own numb brain fixed on one thought. *I want you 'til forever, Rory Drummond, and maybe 'til the day after that.*

They walked together to the ranch house, both silent, their fingers entangled. Still feeling the phantom flutters in his ass, Alex began to suffer the cramping in his gut he'd begun to experience every time he thought about what he was doing here, on a dream hunt to his past. With a man he was supposed to spy on. A man he was also, *por Diós*, falling in love with.

Before they got to the house, Rory stopped and squeezed his hand a little. "A crowned thistle, lad."

*Five Scottish pence for your thoughts.*

Alex could think only of the truth to tell this awakener of dreams. "You, Rory. Just you."

The shivering cold and the thought of missing Steve's gala stopped him from leading Rory back to the cabin and telling him everything from the beginning. Begging his forgiveness, confessing his confused feelings of love.

But it was cold and growing colder; and he could hear the whoops of laughter and sounds of music from the ranch house.

"C'mon, Rory. Let's go get good and drunk."

# Chapter Twelve
## Devil Whisky

*Thank God for this "buddy system." Alex, lad, sometimes you need me more than you'll admit.*

He let Alex lean against him heavily until they were free of the eyes of the party-goers in the ranch house; and then he scooped him up and carried him with sure steps, even in the dark, back to their wooded haven.

He laid the tall man across the bed, leaving him just long enough to find the gas lamp and then turn on the space heater. Kneeling at his lover's feet, he removed the boots first, his fingers and thumbs caught up in a mile of laces. He laid the Timberlands, then the heavy stockings, in a neat pile at the side of the bed.

Rory fumbled with the buttons of his handsome western-style shirt, until he discovered the counterfeit buttons were really cunning snaps. Grinning in satisfaction, he pulled until he heard a *pop-pop-pop* of heavy cotton opening to his touch, saw Alex's ripe nipples nested in dark hair.

*I want every shirt from now on to have snaps, like this. Or velcro. Something my bloody fingers don't have to learn, like truant schoolboys. So I can get to those nipples.*

By now he knew intimately how to undo the metal button of the Levi's. After unzipping them and pulling them over his lover's now-bare feet, he stood back a little and let his eyes devour Alex's inert body. The swelling muscles, the veins running like rivers in an alien landscape against the dusky silk of his skin. The thick cock, now lying almost docile, yet never tamed, in the dark coils of his pubic hair.

*Alex, Alejo. By God, lad, you are young, vulnerable. But somehow you are come here to be my foogin savior. I feel it.*

"Rory ... I am sorry..."

Alex was tossing his head from side to side, trying to apologize for drinking too much. Hell, the man deserved to let go a little, drink enough to get on-his-ass drunk for once. He needed to be taken from his death-grip on the steering wheel of a policeman's vehicle, to a place of freedom. He needed to be pursued, to be lusted after. To be loved.

He heard his own voice, husky with emotion, assuring his lover. "It's all right, Alejo. Worry not, lad. Every man needs to loose the devil's grip on his dry throat." He sat next to him and began to run his hand lightly across the man's parchment skin, from the hollow of his throat to his navel.

His voice thick with whisky, Alex was clearly drunk as a laird. "You don't understand. I'm sorry. I'm a fucking fraud. You need to forget ... forget—"

Rory cupped his cobwebby chin, just beginning to grow a midnight beard, nestling the dear face in his own rough hands. He leaned and kissed him lightly. "Forget you? Nay, never. *No, mi caro. Te quiero.* Sleep for me, will you?"

He managed to pull the quilt from beneath Alex's inert body and tuck it around him. Then, still fully dressed, he lay next to him, one arm over his chest, feeling the steady rise and fall of his breath.

Alex had seemed fine earlier today, actually up until the time they entered Steve's ranch house. Maybe it was the crush of strangers in the dining room and on the deck, so many people talking, laughing, singing. He thought Alex certainly did not get out much. Perhaps the social scene was a bit frightening, even to a crusty cop. Or especially to a cop, who naturally would hold himself free from glad-handers and casual gatherings.

Alex had accepted a glass of whisky from Steve and had tossed it down immediately, the same as he himself had often done when he was either upset or too excited. He'd turned away from his lover, loath to fuss over him. And yet every time he rejoined Alex, he seemed to be just finishing another glass, teetering a little even in his sensible boots midway through the evening, finally toward the end leaning heavily against the rail on the deck.

An hour or so into the welcoming party, after Alex had refused to eat any of the delicacies laid out on the expansive table, Rory had started to worry a little. He remembered gently teasing him, wanting the man to line his stomach with some kind of food before applying too much alcohol to his gut.

"Alex, let's sit and eat together. You need to explain to me, what are 'beanie weenies'? And how the foog does a man eat a 'lady-finger'?"

Alex had merely looked deep into his eyes and lifted his glass. His declaration was solemn, words of a man deep in drink, not intentionally humorous. "I love weenies. I love *your* weenie. So where would I put a lady's finger? I'll be fine, man. Grab a bite to eat. I'll be right here."

An hour later, he'd excused himself to Steve, cupped Alex's elbow, guided him onto the front porch; and from there they'd made it back to their cabin.

And now he lay wide awake, trying to puzzle out Alex's words a while ago. *I'm a fucking fraud. You need to forget—*

*Forget what, love? Forget your getting drunk? That's easy. Forget we ever met? Not in the lifetime of this universe.*

And what did he mean, that he was a "fraud"? Just as Rory had called himself a "lummox," he thought Alex's confession might be a kind of self-deprecation, a way of apologizing for his impoverished emotional life, or maybe for his lack of experience... Bloody hell, he couldn't even begin to guess why a man would have such a low opinion of himself.

He decided Alex needed to hear, early and often, how goddamn sexy he was, how desirable, how smart and capable. He was sure no one had told him that, ever. He imagined Alex's long-dead father had loved his son, and he probably had let him know it. But with both parents dead all those years, and no lover in sight, who would whisper the truth, the words he needed to hear?

*I will, lad. I promise, only the truth.*

When he opened his eyes, the room was almost dark. The lamp had guttered out for lack of fuel. He felt the warmth from Alex's body all along his own, and he saw the orange glow of the heating elements in the small appliance on the floor a few feet away.

"Rory."

He pressed his arm a little into Alex's chest, a gesture of reassurance.

"What, love?"

"I disappointed you. And I'm fucking sorry."

He smiled into the shadow that was their bed. "Never, Alejo. I'll tell you the shame of it. I rather enjoyed carrying you, taking care of you. I should be the one apologizing, A grown man does not need a wet nurse, eh?"

"I don't know what got into me."

"About half a bottle of whisky, lad. You'll piss it out soon enough. And then it will be no more than a bloody bad dream. Hold me, will you?"

Alex fought the swaddling clothes a little, finally freeing his arms, wrapping them around his shoulders. "I need to tell you..."

Rory waited, letting his lover form the words, aching to hear his secret and yet frightened of his own response. *What if this man feels ... something deep ... for me, as I feel for him? Am I ready to share it?*

After a while, he realized Alex had fallen back to sleep, his warm breath fanning his throat, his hands clasped between his shoulder blades.

At last he, too, felt the lure of sleep. The last thing he remembered was the sensation of Alex raising his head, his lips closing on the underside of his jaw beneath the beard, a brief lapping of warm tongue, a burrowing of his head again into the hollow of his throat.

\*\*\*\*

He woke with a splitting headache, a mouth full of sour cotton, and a hunk of redwood timber between his legs.

Alex's first thought was, *Today we start the hunt*. And his second thought was, *No way, José.*

He was aware of Rory's heavy body pressed into his bladder, one massive leg pinning his thighs to the bed. He tried to slide free without waking his bed mate, needing to relieve a piss hard-on that needed either to hang over the rustic toilet bowl or drive up his lover's butt. The state of his mouth and his head told him to try for the toilet first. And then after relieving himself, if he was lucky, he'd enter Rory anyway while he slept.

He struggled to the can and took a good five minutes trying to soften the wood no lumberjack could chop. *Holy shit, I must have rubbed against Rory all night long, to get my dick this excited.*

Finally he was able to take a leak, and as he made his way back across the splintery floor in bare feet, he remembered his actions last night and stood rock-still, cursing himself.

*Steve must think I'm a fucking drunk. And Rory ... he has to be disgusted with me. I thought I could hold my liquor. What the hell happened to me?*

And then it came back. His remorse at the shitty assignment the governor had saddled him with. His own cowardice in not admitting the truth to a man he respected. More than respected, fuck, he was ass-over-cock infatuated with. And his brilliant solution? To get so shit-faced drunk he didn't have to think about it for a while. Until he didn't remember, didn't feel guilty, didn't frigging care for a few oblivious hours.

He stood near the heater, looking at Rory sprawled on the bed. Hell, the man was still fully dressed. Had he gotten drunk too? The memory came back in waves of remorse: Rory half-assed carrying him, laying him down, undressing him, stroking him from throat to belly. Talking, murmuring, saying impossibly tender things...

The thought hit him with an abruptness that almost toppled him: *I do not deserve Rory Drummond. A man of depth, compassion, honesty. And love. Next to him, I'm a fucking fraud. I need to leave now, before I can do any more damage to an honorable man.*

The tears had already threatened a few times lately, and now they welled in the corners of his eyes, acrid and harsh, a reminder of his fucking miserable life, of the promise he was letting slip away.

*Because why? Because I agreed to a crappy job for a freaking politician? Because my job is more important than a man I could cherish the rest of my life? Because I'm a goddamn coward, not worth his slightest consideration.*

He tried to swallow, found his throat full of the taste of bitter whisky, swallowed anyway. Turning from the heater and returning to the little toilet, he vomited and cried at the same time.

When he finally padded back toward the bed, Rory was sitting on the edge, his brows furrowed. Not angry. Alex could tell he was confused, maybe. And definitely upset.

"Alex, lad. You're sick."

"Fucking A, Rory. Sick of being a drunk. Sick of being a goddamn loser."

Rory stood up, eyes blazing thunderbolts. For the first time, Alex felt more than a little daunted by the big guy. "Stop it. I don't want to hear bloody bullshit." He grabbed both shoulders, held on even though Alex tried to twist away from his grasp.

He couldn't even look at Rory, needed to finish throwing up, dress, and maybe leave for good. He couldn't remember ever feeling this full of remorse, even after being abandoned by one foster home and hustled to another in the dead of night, clutching a tiny bag holding every goddamn thing a kid held dear... His mind clamped shut on memories too bleak to revisit.

"Listen to me. No loser ever won Rory Drummond. Never. You are the man I ... I want so much it hurts my foogin heart. Understand? You are the winner I always looked for. The one—goddamn bloody hell, lad. Grow a set of bollocks and look me in the eyes."

He raised his head, fighting for control of the tears that had not dried, inwardly cursing his weakness. At this moment, his lover's face seemed hewn in stone, his mouth rigid, nostrils wide as a bullock's.

The eyes were what held him. Chips of jade, hard, unblinking.

"I was not going to revile you, Alex Dominguez. Every man needs to visit the cups, toss down a few. And some don't know when to stop. But you—you're no drunk. We both know that. And you're no loser. So why are you behaving like a bloody child? A child needs to be turned over my knee. Is that what you want? Tell me?"

"Fuck you."

"I bloody *will* fuck you, lad, and more besides. After I'm through with you, your ass will whimper and snivel for a week."

Alex tried to turn in his hard grasp, but the man picked him up by the upper arms, backed up a foot, and sat on the edge of the bed, all the while twisting him until he lay across his lap. Alex began to kick and buck, intent on escaping what he knew would be part sex game, part ruthless intent.

The first strike brought fresh tears to his eyes and a jolt up his ass, a shudder of stinging hurt that sang like a choir of demons. "No!" He heard his own strident voice, drowned in the next instant by another resounding smack across both buttocks.

"You." *Slap!* "Will. Listen to me." *Smack!* "I'll blister your butt 'til you come in my lap. Understand?"

Rory was right, as usual. Even through the stinging pain, his cock and his asshole seemed joined to a buzz saw that rasped and hummed until he wanted nothing more than to spread his legs and take Rory's big prick all the way up, both of them spitting cum for fucking ever.

He felt himself picked up again, then thrown onto the bed surface, face down. A fumbling of material, a cursing of *foogin buttons* and *bloody zippers*, and Rory's unrelenting cock at the entrance of his hole. His voice grated in his ear. "You're lucky I carry this lube. Otherwise..."

A slick finger entered him, then another. He arced his ass, opened his legs, mutely begging for more. The next sensation was Rory's tongue and mouth, pulling, biting, sucking his hole, slobbering, his words bubbling between his legs. "Open, god damn you. I'm through with your whimpering and whipping yourself."

Hot flesh battered the entrance of his asshole, retreated, rammed again. Alex tried to force his legs wider, willed his rectal clench to relax, until somehow the cock slid inside. He sobbed into the bunched up quilt, the mass of too-hot flesh filling him to the marrow, to the fucking extent of his private haven. The heat grew too intense to bear, his muscles began to rush and tingle in his frenzy to unleash the drowning of *now now now...*

He might have been screaming, or it could have been his lover. It didn't matter. He welcomed Rory's pushing and pummeling until there were only after-shocks to tell him how much he loved this cock, this nirvana, this man.

Rory gathered him to his chest, still sodden and wrinkled in last night's white dress shirt. "Alex. Do not speak. This was a cure for hangover. My special remedy. And when we walk out together, it will be as equals. Rory and Alex. Two winners."

He nodded against the expanse of chest, and Rory held him even tighter. "I'll tell you a secret sometime, Alex Dominguez. Words I've not told any man. Nor will ever tell another. And if you misbehave again, I'll find bloody leather and rope. You'll not escape my wrath. That is what I call making love to my man."

Alex began to laugh into Rory's shirt, nausea forgotten, ass singing, heart hammering. He raised his head and looked at his lover.

Rory was scowling, eyes riveted on his, and his mouth was twisted in his odd smile, one lip curled up almost into his mustache.

"I can hardly wait, you wild-ass Scotsman, until my turn comes around."

"I call myself a Scot, lad. The man part is taken for granted."

When they kissed, it was as tender as their fucking had been a frenzy of lust, until Alex was ready to willing to bury his guilt again in the wonder of Rory Drummond.

# Chapter Thirteen
## The Return

Alex saw immediately two of the new guests were not at the breakfast table; and he wondered how long everyone had hung in last night, drinking and eating and glad-handing. He remembered only a few things: Rory urging him to eat something... Drew whatsisname asking him about being a cop, then following Rory around like a faithful hound... Steve wondering once if he was doing okay, working his way around his big old house getting to know his most recent batch of big game hunters.

As soon as they entered the dining room, Alex sucked in a big breath and approached Steve Long, ensconced in his accustomed chair at the head of the long table.

"Steve. I ... ah, I want to apologize for being an asshole last night."

Steve let his spoonful of oatmeal pause a tick before putting it in his mouth and chewing, shaking his head, frowning a little. Alex waited for the recriminations that never came.

The dark-haired man swallowed his food. "Don't have a clue what you mean, Alex. You need to grab breakfast while it's still hot. You know Moriah won't let go of your gonads unless you're fit to be out there. Full stomach and warm clothes. Period." Then he grinned. "But you know all that. So sit down and eat. Okay?"

He lowered his head again to the bowl of mush, and Alex turned away, relieved. He sat next to Rory, who seemed already at the mercy of Ralph Gore, the man with more.

"...doesn't mean Heart of Ohio can't insure you, Rory. We have clients as far away as Calcutta and Singapore. Honest to God. Be smart with Heart, I always say."

Rory waggled his eyebrows a bit at Alex as he slid next to him, never pausing in his attack on a plate heaped with sausages and eggs. "Aye lad," he mumbled every so often, and "Truly now?"

Alex grinned. He could think of no man who needed insurance less than the competent castle laird, one who exuded more good health and extreme fitness than any man he'd ever met. If anyone needed it, he decided, it was Gore himself, who could probably use about a few months of rib-sticking home-cooked meals.

As they ate, two of the missing guests came in together—straight-haired Drew and the Texan, Sam, the one he decided looked more like a Russian bear than anything. Alex wondered whether Steve had told everyone last night about the buddy system, decided it really didn't matter. Those two were already friends. And burly Mark, sitting next to the salesman, was clearly going to keep an eye on the skinny dude. He'd seen that from the get-go yesterday at the airport, and later when they were eating together at a fast-food joint.

*Funny how strangers begin to take care of each other without even knowing they're doing it. If it's a common cause.* He'd already learned enough about male bonding in two days to keep him warm for a frigging lifetime. He'd noticed last night Drew already seemed infatuated by Rory, but the big highlander naturally drew most folks' attention. As long as the dude didn't try to share their bed, he didn't really much care.

Halfway through the meal, Steve tapped his spoon on his coffee mug. "Gentlemen. In three hours, say around ten, please be prepared to take off for the first leg of our hunt. We'll be going to our base camp in vehicles, getting a feel for the land, selecting our weapons. We'll hear a few words from Jack and some of the boys about safety and rules of the trail. Maybe even spot a few mulies, who knows?"

He set the spoon down and took a swig of coffee. "Please, fellas. Keep eating. All I want to say is: Dress warm. Layer your clothes, even your underwear. Maybe especially your underwear, and your feet. It's not cold yet. But the higher we go, the more your balls will feel it. And your toes."

Jack looked around the table. "If you fellows have any questions, ask away."

"Will we be staying there tonight?" Drew wanted to know.

"Yep. You'll put up your own tent, two men to a tent. Buddies bunk together."

Gore seemed a little nervous. "Do we have to carry a lot of supplies up the mountain? Not sure I'm that strong."

In answer, Zeb shook his head, and Jack went back to his sausage. "We'll have pack horses for the weapons and supplies. Bring along what you can't live without, no more. When we really start to tracking, everyone will get a light backpack and their chosen rifle. Can't go back down to base camp every time we want to toast marshmallows."

Everyone laughed, even Steve, when Gore said, "Damn, fellas, what am I gonna do with my recipe for s'mores?"

Jack chuckled. "You just worry about getting your trophy. We'll worry about the food and gear. Okay?"

After breakfast, walking back to the cabin with Rory, Alex experienced the first trickles of excitement from his nape down his backbone, the same sensation he used to feel before his father took him for their one- or sometimes two-week excursions to the mountain.

It would start the night before, packing their warmest clothing in backpacks, rolling stuff just right to make sure everything was layered according to when they'd use it. Mom helping with the dried food and utensils, shaking her head in mock despair when she found no toothbrush at the top of the pack.

"You will have to smell each other's breath, *hijo*, all night long. *Piedad*. Lord have mercy on both of you."

The memory, like an elusive bird, fluttered at the back of his mind before settling in his smile. "Damn, Rory. I feel almost like a kid again. Just the idea of tasting the first air of Moriah, touching her snowdrifts ... seeing the aspens and the pines..."

Rory stopped and looked around, then briefly touched his cheek, ran his thumb from his jaw to his chin. "I can tell, lad. The look in your eyes. I wish I could catch it like a firefly in a bottle. I love looking at you at this moment. And later, on the mountain ... I think you'll feel even better."

Alex smiled and ducked his head a little, knowing they were in plain sight of any of their new hunting buddies who might be walking to their own cabin. "Come on. Race you to the cabin." *Because I want to fuck you in a real bed before we have to do it in a tent, on a rock, in a snowbank.*

\*\*\*\*

Almost at base camp, after an hour of rattling along in a four-wheel drive Jeep, Rory felt his ass begin to complain. *Suspension like a foogin Russian tractor. I'll take my gelding Duffy any day. Ah, my castle for a horse.*

They had drawn one of the wranglers as driver, a competent young man named Tommy. Two other vehicles were behind them—another Jeep and an older model four-passenger Chevrolet Trailblazer. The rest of Steve's men were leading pack horses, and both Jack and Zeb had gone ahead to make sure the road was clear of any surprises the recent storm might have deposited on the road.

"Are we there yet?"

Next to him, squeezed between him and the driver, Rory glanced over with a slight grin and managed to move his right hand furtively on his inner thigh. "The place we're going is one my father and I used to use. From there, halfway up the mountain, we'll be close to Hendry's Creek trail, one of the best ways to scale Moriah. It follows the creek bed, no doubt frozen by now. But it's the same one I'm used to. Not so tough these boys can't follow it. But kind of a challenge if you're not used to the altitude."

"How high is Moriah, lad?"

"It stands twelve thousand feet. And our camp is at roughly seventy-five. Enough to let us know we're definitely in the Snake Range."

"Damn, lad, the tallest of the Cairngorms is less than five thousand of your Yankee feet. Ah, but the sea is scant miles away. So we're talking the distance from sea level. My own mountains seem to be this high, this rugged ... because they are. As the eagle flies from wave to summit."

"I'd like to see them someday, Rory."

"I think you will." *If I can move other mountains, lad, I'll make sure you see them. And soon.*

Alex cocked one eyebrow. "Oh? And how would a Nevada State Trooper move his butt from here to there?"

"On a magic carpet. How the foog do I know? I just know."

Their driver pulled into a relatively open area, one bounded by a kind of split-log fence but made entirely of stout timbers. A sign that might have been fifty years old bore the words "Moriah Wilderness Camp One."

Tommy braked but kept the engine running. "Time to get our tails wet, boys. Get out here while I park, wouldya?"

Within a few moments, the six hunters stood with Steve Long, looking around at their new accommodations. Rory saw there was plenty of room to pitch tents next to a line of sheltering junipers and white pines; and that's where Tommy was parking the Safari while the other two vehicles were pulling in at the same time. He immediately felt the wind moving from the highlands and instinctively began to walk to the lee side of the clearing and toward the trees.

He turned and announced, "Don't mind me, lads. 'Tis time to greet Mother Nature." He walked into the trees and pissed long and hard into a snowbank that still clung to the north side of a tall pine. Standing with his legs wide apart and his head flung back, he spoke aloud to the intense blue sky. "Damn, I missed this. It feels like home."

Half an hour later, six wranglers with pack horses had arrived, and Paul was busy unloading food supplies into a cook tent he and a few others had erected right away. Twenty feet from the tent, Steve had all the new hunters, along with Jack and Zeb, helping build a large cookfire.

Steve looked up from the new fire and grinned at his charges.

"Okay, my men have unloaded your tents. Time to get 'em set up. Afterwards, you can pile your private stuff inside. Even take a break while Paul and his crew fix lunch. Then we'll talk turkey."

Rory wondered what "talk turkey" meant, decided it had nothing to do with his new favorite whisky, crooked his upper lip and one eyebrow in a signal to Alex.

They walked together to a pile of identical tents. They were smallish, lightweight but durable. Rory reckoned each one would be about right for one to three men, dome tents designed to be erected quickly. He and Alex bent and together picked up one of them, a green-and-white polyfiber affair that was light but bulky. Bundled in the tent was a set of six heavy-duty tent stakes. There was only one sturdy mallet lying next to the pile of tents, and Rory wanted to seize it immediately.

He turned to his partner. "Pick your spot, lad."

"Away from the rest."

"Then we'll have to wait until everyone else has taken their choice of location. No matter. Privacy is worth the wait."

"Rory, now that I think about it ... how private can we be? In a thin tent with only a four foot high flap to shield our naked asses?"

"'Tis the thought, Alex. We can take our promised walk together while everyone puts up their new domicile."

He piled their tent and stakes next to a middle-aged pine whose needles had already carpeted the snow-covered ground at its base. "Come. Show me your heart, lad."

Alex smiled at him, his eyes deeper and more full of dancing lights than he'd ever seen them. "I'd like to show you more than that. Let's just behave ourselves, okay? Come with me."

"Come with you? Always, I hope." His voice was grave, but his intentions were very foogin frisky. He could hardly wait to walk out of sight of the others and kiss Alex on his sensuous, pouty lower lip.

"Let me clear it with Steve, okay?"

Rory nodded, glad Alex had thought of it. It would be stupid to bound away like a couple of rabbits when Steve was rightfully concerned about everyone's safety. He thought he could almost hear the older man talking. "Stay close. Keep to the road. Don't let your butts be a target for some asshole with a hunting rifle." Later, when he and Alex had proved their abilities to cope with this majestic lady Moriah, he'd be less like a mother hen.

Alex joined him at the tall pine, his eyes shining. "Steve just said be back in half an hour."

They walked together up the road they had just come from, the part no vehicle had taken lately. If the recent storm had left a rockslide or a pile of detritus, they would turn around and come back.

A few minutes into their walk, Rory reached over and took Alex's left hand. "Talk to me, lad. I want to know this lady Moriah. I want to see a glimpse of you and your father among those trees."

They walked side by side for a while, Alex apparently sorting through memories, deciding what to tell him.

"It was usually this time of year, Rory. October's first snowfall would have brought the mulies, even a few elk, down from the treeline, following the browse under snowdrifts. Father would be a little ahead, scouting the trail, looking for pellets maybe. I'd stop every ten minutes or so and use the binocs. Patient as a kid could be ... which was pretty goddamn jittery, wanting to catch up to him, run next to him. Not have to walk in his deep boot prints."

Rory stopped, wanting to watch Alex's face as he talked.

"Not that I could begin to fill those tracks back then, Rory. I was young and dumb, but I knew I wanted to be just like him. Humble and ... and loving and faithful... Strong."

Rory bent so his face was inches away from his lover's.

"You are all those things, Alex Dominguez. Your father's child. Completely."

"I loved him so fucking much..."

Rory embraced him, letting the dark head lean on his chest. When he tipped Alex's chin up to his own and lightly kissed him, he could taste a saltiness he'd have been disappointed not to find on his full lips. "I know. I feel that love."

They kissed again, this time with growing passion. Alex's fingers seized the back of his head, trailed through his hair, then down his throat, to the front of his jacket, until they rested on the straining denim of the Levi's crotch.

Rory licked and pulled Alex's lower lip, then grabbed his cheeks and began to plunder his mouth, his tongue taking no prisoners.

"Alex, I need you. Today, tomorrow, always. Will you?" He was speaking into his lover's mouth, needing to bring him even closer.

Alex pulled away a little and looked into his eyes, his expression full of passion and ... was it regret?

"I want to. Honest to God, Rory. I want to."

"What's the matter Alex? Are you already married? Who's the other man? I swear I'll kill him—"

Alex laughed and seized his hand, pulled him along the road with him. "Let's live in this moment, okay? You, the mountains, the promise of—I don't know. Something great. Walk with me. Just be with me."

Rory let those words warm him for the next little while, as they followed a road only memory could make more beautiful.

Keenly aware of the altitude, he drew the thin air into his chest, slow and deep, as he walked. Each side of the narrow road was still partly snow-covered, the small rounded tufts revealing their true identity on the south side—the ubiquitous sage brush he'd read about. He also noticed stands here and there of some kind of wide-bladed grass showing pale green and yellow where the snow was thinnest.

The midday sun seemed to ricochet crystal nuggets from the landscape. He walked in silence, watching always for the sight of a shy head, a pair of antlers, a slender tawny neck to emerge from the tree cover.

He knew enough about the foraging habits of deer to know the creatures would be making their way down from the higher elevations, where deeper snow would have buried the most succulent browse. But they would also stay close to the line of trees. No mulie would resist the juvenile needles of junipers, and he noticed the lower limbs of those trees already betrayed the recent trace of hungry deer.

Their own big-game hunting party couldn't be the only one to come through here recently. So the deer would seek the sheltering trees, bolt nervously into the safety of needles and branches at the slightest sound or unfamiliar scent. The thrill of the hunt began to creep along the nape of his neck, the old feeling of tracking something alien, surpassingly graceful and elegant, untouchable in its mystery.

He was content to walk with his lover, changing direction downhill to camp when Alex silently turned back. Thinking of his boundless attraction to this dark-eyed man, he was sorry when the sound of distant laughter filtered through the trees .

He squeezed Alex's hand and let it go. They shared one long look, full of secrets, and then walked back to what he could only call foogin civilization.

## Chapter Fourteen
### Gang Warily

On the road, walking hand in hand with his lover, he watched and listened for the young Alejo to come bounding through the trees. Alex thought his heart would burst as he shared some of his vision with Rory. And he was sure the big Scot, his eyes bright with understanding, was seeing it too.

The voice of Ramón had come back to him for the first time in ten years. "*Hijo.* You must always be so aware of everything around you, nothing can surprise you. Even the soft eyes of a doe watching from a stand of mountain mahogany. *Sí? Comprendes?* And when you walk, let it be with care and understanding ... with knowledge. Like seeing everything and knowing it well. Before *it* can know *you*."

His father had taught him slowly, his words like pitch oozing from a white pine, and every day had held some wonder. He remembered as he walked, just how much of what he'd learned had become part of his everyday breathing and seeing and thinking.

Today Alex knew, more keenly than ever in his life, how his father's patient love had prepared the boy for losing him. Prepared him to become a man. During the four years of gut-deep anguish, being shuffled from one set of parched hearts to the next, he'd somehow survived okay.

He'd managed to be on time for his classes every day. He'd been able to remember everything the teachers said, even reading after school as he walked back to what the state agency people had called "home." He wouldn't be allowed to study once he closed the door to the alien house, so he relied on his memory and his inborn cunning. So his grades were good, sometimes even outstanding, in spite of the neglect.

He'd built up his body in secret, certain his closeted attraction to men would bring trouble if he couldn't defend himself. He'd been patient, letting the pain lie too deep to pull out and examine. And now, all of a sudden, it was all bubbling to the surface. Not just the tamped-down pain, but the stifled love too. What was happening to him?

He'd stopped feeling love as soon as his parents had died, up until a few days ago. Until this moment, actually.

No sense shutting out the healing, the way he'd shut out the hurt. Just walking along a freaking road halfway up Mt. Moriah, on a day when the sun was melting patches of snow and warming the frigid ground, on this astonishing day as he held the large warm hand of a remarkable man, he knew he could love someone. He was almost sure someone loved him, at long last.

Back in camp, he and his lover laughing and putting up the tent, trying to stake it down when the wind had begun to change direction into the trees ... later, squatting at the large cook fire, eating beans and franks off a bent metal plate ... standing around with the other hunters, listening to Jack and Zeb talk about trail safety ... fingering a handsome Ruger medium-range rifle, claiming it, already squinting through the scope... All of it was a freaking dream he wanted never to wake from.

And when night fell, when a dozen or so rowdy men were squatting and guffawing around the large fire, he felt happier than he had in damn near half a lifetime. He and Rory walked to their tent, listening to the wail of a harmonica cry out to the cold stars. Once away from the fire, he reached for the man's hand as they sought their tent, pitched well back into the trees, a small clearing Rory had made their own.

Like half of each buddy team, Rory wielded a flashlight so they could find their night's rest without suffering a pratt-fall or twisted ankle. Alex knew even as he pulled the flap loose that the ground temps were below freezing. They would emphatically not be exposing their bare butts tonight. But it didn't matter. They'd work around it.

Every minute alone with Rory Drummond was a call to the passionate impulses Alex had hidden his entire adult life. He'd already found he couldn't be within a few feet of the man without having to hide an erection—or, if they were alone, give in to it. And he surrendered to it now, as Rory followed him into the place of privacy.

They had demurely claimed two sleeping bags. Yet Alex was sure they'd use the large one to lie in and the smaller as double insulation. Without taking off a shred of clothing, Rory settled down in the sleeping bag, and Alex slid in next to him. Both of them had unbuttoned and unzipped their denims, but with the freeze sitting like judgment all around them, they naturally rolled tight together, crotch to crotch, and began to kiss.

Rory's tongue was down his throat immediately, and Alex began to suck, in a tempo he echoed with his hips, driving his hard-on into his lover's groin ... retreating, advancing again, his stiff flesh ramming into a cock already slick with early cum.

"Alex. I want to suck you." Rory was eating the hollow of his throat, his bulk reared above him, the cold air penetrating their tousled sleeping gear.

"And I want you to. Do it, do it."

How did the large man end up with his head between Alex's eager thighs? He didn't know, and he didn't care. As often as they'd made love, it had always ended with one of their dicks up the other man's ass. Being sucked off ... well, he could think of less pleasant ways to spend this night. He laughed softly at his own thought, until he felt his entire cock being slicked into an endless hot throat, and then he gasped with the intensity and sweetness of it.

"God, Rory..."

Rory's large hands were cupping his butt cheeks, raising his groin high, higher, until he let his entire body relax into the sensation of a soft beard against his own pubic hair, a tongue wandering from his balls to his tip, then another fast immersion into an inferno of deep throat.

"I need you, Alejo." A finger slid into his asshole, then two more, slick with ... something. Spit or lube or pre-cum, he didn't care, spreading his legs as much as he could to accept the stiff intrusion while the tongue played with his gooch and balls, then returned to his shaft.

"Eat me." He heard his own moan rise, tried to choke back the scream waiting in his throat, knowing everyone in camp would hear his rampant need.

*Now.* He arced, the fingers reaching deeper. Now. His entire body stiffened, concentrating the sensation into the white-hot center of his deep ass and his hard balls. The charge exploded up his ass and out his slit; and he cried out loud, like a kid, sobbing while the tide took him somewhere far away.

Rory laid his lower body down and crawled back up to join him.

"Your turn, Rory." He began to stroke his lover's nape and throat, then the fawn-soft beard.

"Nay. Later. I want you to tell me bed-time stories. Will you?"

By now he was drowsy, indolent in the aftermath of satisfaction, wanting to please his lover yet wobbly-brained on the edge of sleep.

"Anything. What should I tell you?"

"About Alejo. *El hijo de su padre*, his father's son."

He lay with his mouth just below the soft earlobe, brushing it every so often with his tongue. It seemed to him he talked for an hour, though it could have been five minutes, or fifteen. The way his father had taught him to see every leaf on a tree, the tremble of every needle. The way he'd learned to open his ears to the cry of the birds as they soared or flitted overhead. His caution, his abandon. His songs and his stories.

"When he left me, and my mother soon after, there was just a deep hole, Rory. And into that hole the fucking nightmares settled."

The memories were impressions, actually. Of hard eyes, rough hands, flat voices. Shouts and recriminations when they found him and his foster brother together. Or when they found him reading under the covers with a stolen flashlight. Or a thousand other unforgivable transgressions. Hours of sitting in darkness while the food was withheld. Never physical punishment, only mental. Four years of it, as though one set of pretend parents had written instructions for the next.

As he spoke, Rory's arms tightened around him. Yet he never said a word.

Now close to sleep, Alex murmured something he had to tell Rory. "It's all come back now. Out of my gut, into the open. And that's good. I needed it all to come out. Not just my father, but the other stuff too. Does that even make sense?"

"It does, lad."

"Can you accept a guy so fucked up? Whose head is still wrapped around old memories?"

"More than that, Alex." Rory reared up a little on one elbow, reaching for something, maybe in his pocket. After a minute, he pressed something into his hand.

"When you were talking about your father, what he taught you, I remember something my own father taught me. Gave me. And I want to share it with you. Put it away. Look at it tomorrow. Or a week from now. Think of it as ... as a troth."

He felt the roundness of something, like a coin, and he put it in his jeans pocket so he wouldn't lose it in the folds of the sleeping bag.

"What the fuck is a 'troth,' Rory?"

His lover chuckled. "Something Scots and knights in armor say. Not important. Just know we have a bond."

"Bond. James Bond."

Rory laughed with real humor. "Something like that. And because we have a bond, I'll ask for my half tomorrow." He nuzzled Alex's throat, just under the jaw, pulling him closer.

"Before breakfast?" He was almost asleep, but teasing Rory felt damn good.

"As soon as I wake up, lad. Because I know I'll greet the morning with the devil's own wood."

\*\*\*\*

Before the sun had hardly ventured over the cold peaks of the Snake Range, six would-be hunters, stomachs full of flapjacks and coffee, were on the trail of their prey, along with a Long Trails crew of six. Rory looked around appraisingly at the party. Steve was leading the climb along with Jack, his head man, both of them bearing their hunting rifles on a strap over heavy jackets. He and Alex followed not too far behind. Each of them was trying to walk subtly abreast, but the trail was beginning to narrow.

He waved Alex ahead of himself, wanting to keep an eye on him yet not betraying that fact. "You're younger, lad. I'll try to keep up with you, a step behind."

Alex had grinned and winked, not fooled by his tactic. The man was watching over him. Or maybe he was remembering the scene in the sleeping bag this morning when Rory had awakened him with a cattle prod to his buttocks, with a prick rigid as a tent stake.

He glanced back from time to time. The other four hunters were strung out by a distance of twenty or so feet, sometimes walking two by two as he and Alex had been, other times singly. He heard Mark now and then muttering to his partner Gore. "Careful there, fella." ... "Best keep your eyes on the trail." ... "Don't try to walk too fast. Slow, steady, okay?"

Zeb was climbing steadily, sometimes joining him and Alex, other times pausing to banter a moment with the others. Rory saw right away, Zeb was what they called a "trouble shooter" on the American westerns he loved to watch. He was the one trained to observe any potential danger or misstep by Gore and Drew, the two mostly-novice climbers. Three other Long Trails men were at the back of the group. The rest of the ranch crew were the camp cooks or other handlers, back at base camp, already preparing food for the returning men or taking care of the pack animals.

Steve had decided to strike out for a prominent outcropping about fifteen hundred feet from base camp. From there, he'd told them, they'd be able to survey a rather wide swath of flatland and bordering trees. If deer were doing early foraging, they'd be able to spot them with binocs from that height.

Rory appreciated Steve's way of handling the men. A brief talk yesterday about the importance of simple safety rules, along with a brush-up on tracking techniques. And then he'd remained basically hands off, not acting like an overseer at all. But the man had eyes of a goshawk. Rory was convinced Steve could see and interpret the movements of every one of the men, and even of the wildlife whose haunts they were hiking through.

A good man, and true. He thought again how fortunate he'd been to choose Steve's ranch for his sojourn. Otherwise, he would never have found the man he intended to claim as his own. He trained his eyes on Alex, walking with a sureness of stride and the balance of a martial artist. The man he'd finally admitted to himself he had fallen in love with.

They were skirting the edge of a long strand of white pines, some towering thirty or forty feet above them, every branch laden with the recent snow. Rory found the sight both lovely and disturbing, as though those grand trees, giants as they were, were forced to carry a harsh burden. A reminder that nature could be cruel as well as beautiful. All through the entire line of trees he saw a steady weeping, snow melting and falling like raindrops as the sun rose higher.

Alex glanced back at him over his shoulder. "Taking a wiz."

"Gang warily." Calling out to Alex, he intentionally echoed the words engraved on the token he'd given him last night, words that came easily to him. *Go with care.* That was the motto of his clan, nine hundred years old, maybe older. The crest Alex now owned bore those words above the figure of a goshawk, proud symbol of Clan Drummond. Giving his lover the circular gold crest had been Rory's way of bringing him into his family. When the enigmatic man finally understood that, the bond would be sealed.

Would Alex recognize the intent? Rory decided he could wait until his lover was ready to see what lay in his heart.

He held back, let the party get ahead of him, watching his partner. Alex zig-zagged around a few snowdrifts, walking on slick ground, as he headed for a nearby pine. Rory idly wondered why every man sought an object to piss against or into. Maybe so the wind wouldn't bring it back around somehow. Americans had a word for it: *hard-wired.* He guessed even Neanderthals had pissed against some random rock wall.

Alex stood for a few moments while Rory fixed the tall, handsome figure in his mind. *He's come here to reunite with his father, and by God I think he's grown an inch in a few days. Everywhere it counts.*

His grin froze as he watched a cascade begin over Alex's head, a toppling and drowning and crashing of snow. To his horrified eyes, it seemed to take place in slow motion, an avalanche no one could have expected. Within seconds, perhaps a ton of snow had given up its place on the tree branches and fallen to the forest floor, each tier falling to the next, lending its weight, adding to the deadly force.

Alex was suddenly buried under a mountain of snow.

Rory hardly remembered throwing off his rifle, running faster than he thought he could, plowing through snowbanks and ground ice to reach his lover. He heard a roaring in his ears, a bellow of pain. By the time he got to Alex, he recognized the sound as his own voice.

He knew of course where Alex had been—within inches of the trunk. He began to frantically use his arms like paddles, throwing snow off to the side. Alex had stood close to the trunk, where there might be pockets of precious air under the huge mound of snow.

He heard himself again, not his own voice but a strangled croak. "Lie still, Alex. Try to breathe slow, lad." Rory had no idea how long he burrowed, throwing snow out of the way, talking to Alex.

"It's all right, lad. I'm almost there."

And then four men, then five or six, had joined him, everyone digging. And within a few minutes, Rory saw the dark blue of his jacket and the green of his hiking boots. Then his Ruger rifle butt. He was on Alex in a beat of his heart, picking him up from the slick, heavy snow and carrying him to the trail.

Steve was kneeling alongside Rory as he helped his lover sit up. By now the entire party was squatting in a circle around the three of them. Drew was snapping pictures again with his annoying little digital camera.

Steve looked worried. "Alex, are you okay? Do you feel dizzy? Any broken bones?"

He was breathing fine, Rory thought, but taking his time to recover his dignity. "I fucked up, didn't I?"

"No." Steve shook his head. "I screwed up by my own oversight. Just because it never happened before, doesn't mean it will never happen. An avalanche can start in a tree. All it takes is a little morning sun, a gradual melting. Like a domino effect. Now we know. Can you stand up?"

"Hell, yeah. Not to worry. I'm fine."

Rory met his eyes. Alex was frightened, he saw that. And gratified. But there was something else reflected there, an emotion he'd never seen on any man's face ... not any man looking at him, and that was a fact.

He smiled, feeling his cheeks ache with the brittle cold in the cracks of his skin. "Don't try to talk yet, lad. I'll unbury your rifle. Let's go stalk a deer."

# Chapter Fifteen
## The Shoot

He was whole—he thought. Except for a few aching muscles and a huge blow to his ego, Alex walked the final seven hundred feet, still ahead of Rory but so aware of him he glanced back often. Each time he did, Rory seemed self-contained, happy, locking eyes with an expression Alex wanted to take to bed with him every night for the rest of his life.

It was more clear to him with every fucking footstep, the gorgeous Scot was taken with him. Infatuated, "ate up with it," as folks say. Not just the way he looked at Alex, but his single-minded frenzy of pulling him from beneath the suffocating snow... Alex could hardly deny there was an emotion riding the man's heart, often whispering, sometimes shouting, telling him he mattered.

Reaching under his long jacket, he felt for and retrieved the strange coin-like object he'd stuffed in his Levi's pocket last night in the dark. He glanced at it as he walked. It was heavy, a circular amulet, dark gold. Some kind of hawk dominated the open center, its claws gripping a crown and its legs fettered by falconer's jesses. The wings were outspread as if to fly, its beak open.

Engraved on the circle surrounding the bird were block letters: *gang warily*. The words scratched at his memory as he put the amulet back in his pocket. Where had he heard them? He'd seen at a glance that Rory had given him a family token, no doubt his own clan crest. The color and weight suggested it was gold, hard enough to engrave—not twenty-four karat, yet still clearly valuable.

As he walked he tried to remember what his lover had said last night. *Think of it as a troth... Something Scots and knights in armor say... A bond.*

And then he remembered where he'd heard the strange words. He'd turned off the trail, hell-bent on finding a tree to wiz against, and Rory's voice had lifted behind him as he damn well forgot his father's caution and his own natural restraint. "Gang warily." It sounded like "gong," maybe the Gaelic word for "go." *Go warily. Be careful.* The sudden insight brought a burn to his face and a renewed cramp to his gut.

Should he have heard the sound of the high snow tower, collapsing of its own weight? Where was the instinct for survival, the still voice he usually heard from some crevice in his brain? At least he'd been close enough to the base of the tree to suck the pockets of air trapped between his head and the tree trunk. He'd used his knowledge of slow-breathing to make the air last, until Rory had found him.

The whole unfortunate accident was another lesson this trip was teaching him. How to reach back and find his father, whose life lessons spoke loud here on their mountain. How to reach inside and find love, for a remarkable man who possibly loved him in return.

Thinking about it, he balled his fists and fought the haze over his eyes. He still hadn't found the strength, the goddamn balls, to confess everything to Rory. Not just his real purpose for being here, but also his growing love.

*If not now, Alex ... when, for God's sake?*

With a real effort, he put it out of his mind for now and concentrated on the trail. To let his mind dwell on guilt was to invite danger all over again.

The bluff where Steve was leading the men was one they could scale from the near side without much strain. Alex consciously relaxed his hunched shoulders and tried to breathe from the diaphragm, bent his legs to adapt to the climb. This time when he glanced back, he saw the entire party was climbing slow but steady, almost at the summit.

When at last they stood at the crest looking into a broad expanse of snowy field and surrounding trees, Alex stood rock still, letting his eyes fill with a scene he remembered even after a dozen years.

A wide valley lay open below, one whose embracing hills were a blaze of aspens and a necklace of deep green pines and lighter green junipers. He knew the aspens shared common root clusters, sometimes stretching for miles, and now that autumn had stolen the green of their leaves, they seemed like tongues of fire. Those trees would be a haven for the wildlife trying to survive, as the cold weather tightened its grip on the mountain.

He'd seen this panorama often, always before with his father. Now he felt another strong presence at his side. He didn't have to turn his head to know Rory was drinking in the scene with him, silent, no doubt as full of wonder as he was. He became aware that one by one, the hunting party was gathering close by to gaze on what Rory always saw as the skirts of Moriah.

He turned to Rory. "She's in her finest dress."

The corners of his eyes crinkled with humor. "To me, she's a wanton showing her bright petticoats. 'Tis a similar vision, lad. Mine just a wee more bit more naughty."

Alex grinned. "I should have known you'd peek under her skirts."

"Only to see if she's hiding a handsome lad between her thighs."

Alex wanted to grab his teasing, handsome lover, take him to the ground, show him all about boys and thighs. His smile widened as he mouthed, "Just fucking wait."

Ten feet away, he heard Steve clear his throat. "Gentlemen. Just a word." The party gathered around to listen.

"Here's where we use our binocs and our powers of observation. This is a prime spot for mulies. When you look at the field, sweep for tracks in the snow. And concentrate on the area along the edge, where the trees meet the open. Our pals will naturally seek a place where they can hide quick if they smell us, or hear us.

"Be patient. A brown deer among those trees is almost invisible, especially from here. But watch for moving shadows where no shadows should be. *Capeesh?*"

Gore spoke up. "What if we see a deer, Steve? Just start shooting, right?"

"Um, pal, we don't have radar range-finders. Just medium-range rifles with scopes. So if we see deer, we're going to try to guess-timate their foraging path. We'll drop lower and try for a shot from around a hundred to a hundred and fifty yards. No wild shooting. Okay?"

Alex was a little annoyed. Ralph Gore was a nice guy, but he was pretty hopeless as a trekker and as a hunter. He hoped his partner Mark would keep him on a short leash. Then he cursed himself for being so hard on the man who was obviously just learning. *Who am I to judge? I'm the guy whose pecker brought down a fucking avalanche.*

All of them lifted their binoculars and began to scan. Alex took his time, starting from the area farthest from their observation spot, almost where the valley started as a jumble of rocks and where the trees were thinnest. He allowed himself to watch the spot for long minutes before moving on, with utmost slowness, knowing what to look for.

He'd seen furtive deer, and elk too, hundreds of times. Yet only a few times had he actually shot one. It was an art to him, not a sport. The art of knowing what your quarry will do and out-maneuvering it. The art of knowing the mind of your prey and out-thinking it.

Steve's words had been spot-on. They'd need to look for a moving shadow, where no shadow should be. He reckoned their guide had taken many a deer in his day. Not necessarily as a trophy, but maybe as a way to survive.

Strangely, he saw the stationary buck before he spotted the moving one. It stood still as a stone, its head lifted. The eight-point antlers were not quite lost among the trees, which were sparse there along the edge where junipers sent their tenacious roots even into fissures in the rocky ground. Another buck, a six-point, walked ten feet farther along, followed by three smaller, younger bucks with single tiers. Now that rutting season was over, he already knew males often foraged together.

He lowered his glasses and laid his hand on Rory's jacket sleeve. "There. Where the valley begins, at the thin line of junipers."

Rory lifted his binocs and took a while to gaze, before letting them hang again from the strap around his neck. "Good eye. They like the tender new juniper growth. I wish we were the only two here, lad. We would take our time, do it right."

*Damn, Rory, I want that too. Take our time, do it right. Just give me another day or so...*

He nodded in agreement. "Steve will make sure of that, I hope. Let me tell him."

A few minutes later, they were all heading toward the place where Alex had seen the mulies, moving more quickly now. He had a feeling that a dozen men scrambling over rocks down a sloping trail were not going to find any deer where he'd just spotted them. They'd be lucky to find any at all. Still, his mind insisted, he wasn't there to bag a deer. Not really. He was there to work out something important that had only a little to do with horns and hide and a lot to do with his own unexplainable self.

\*\*\*\*

Taking his cue from Alex, Rory instantly spotted the small herd of mulies his partner had pinpointed. He took extra time to scan carefully, making sure no others were close by. He made out what seemed to be a trail along the edge of the trees farther south down the valley, perhaps part of the same family.

He and the rest of the hunting party made their way to the bottom, fifteen minutes of descent that made a jest of the hour it had taken to climb, always moving toward their quarry. Steve had told them to fan out in buddy groups, north and south, behind and ahead of the deer, as soon as they got to the valley floor.

He and Alex reached a spot where they could easily stand and take aim if they saw the telltale moving shadows. They were crouched behind a snowbank, actually a large clump of brush whose top had been burned clean of snow by the late morning sun.

His whisper made Alex put his head close to his mouth to hear. "Lad, I give you the first shot."

He felt his lover shake his head, heard his answering husky voice. "No, Rory. Let one of the others go ahead. I like the tracking more than the killing. In fact, I don't like the shooting at all."

He nodded in comprehension. On his deerstalking sojourns, he'd let many a mulie and massive elk bound through the protective trees, simply staring after them, admiring their muscular bodies, the way they moved, flowing ribbons of brown velvet. "Nor do I. In that way, we're brothers in arms." He let a few beats of his heart elapse. "But thank God, not brothers in bed."

Alex flashed a sexy smile, and he felt his cock stiffen, even under the cold embrace of a snow-clad valley. He saw Gore and his partner Mark not fifteen feet away and refrained from kissing his partner's beguiling mouth.

He winked at Alex. "Then who should take first aim?"

"Gore."

They smiled at each other in comprehension. Let the gangly, skinny Ralph Gore claim bragging rights. It would be an unending source of humor to talk about for years to come. If—big if—the guy could put his shot where his mouth was.

Alex signaled him at the same instant he too saw the eight-point. Even without the glasses, he could see the big male a hundred yards to his left grazing the low branches of a young juniper. Still foraging alone, the handsome buck had lifted his head, perhaps out of instinct but more likely due to a movement or a sudden alien scent on the light wind.

Rory made a minuscule "you go ahead" motion and watched Alex inch his way toward their fellow hunters.

Alex crab-walked and bellied through the snow to the other two men, his movements a show of stealth and skill. Rory was sure he was invisible to the stag. He watched him signal to Mark, then to the spot where the buck stood. And then, as clearly as if he were shouting, Alex made it clear that Ralph Gore should take the first shot.

Rory saw Mark's big toothy smile, he saw Gore's uptilted face, and he relaxed back in his squat behind the brush, allowing the mighty hunter to take his prize.

*Blam!*

A rifle shot cracked the still, cold air. Immediately after, a rapid series of rounds sounded fifty feet to his left, where he was certain the six-point and the other three bucks had gone.

Within a few minutes, all five mule deer lay in the snow, their blood already frozen in the packed snow.

He and Alex stood aside while the others clustered around the carcasses. Steve was grinning and congratulating them, explaining they'd leave the mulies here and have some of the boys bring them back on pack animals, dress them later.

Drew insisted on Gore lifting the head of his prize and snapped a few images while the tall, slender man showed the gap in his back molars.

*What makes a man happier ... a rack of antlers, or one charming tail?* He grinned at his own jest, but kept it to himself.

It was time to return to base camp.

Rory felt a sudden urge and spoke quietly to his partner. "Alex, love, guard me while I take a piss. Will you?"

"Guard you from what?"

"Avalanches, lad. And fellow hunters."

He turned and walked a few steps before he heard Alex's voice behind him. "Rory."

He turned and eyed his partner, standing with his legs wide apart and a strange, bemused smile on his face.

"Yes, love?"

"Gang warily."

He could have sworn to God the other man mouthed the word "love" also, but they were too far apart for him to be sure.

## Chapter Sixteen
### The Descent

Alex spent the next three days in the thawing snow on Mt. Moriah, and two nights locked in Rory's arms, fully dressed, on the freezing ground of their tiny tent. He wanted to bottle the experience like fine whisky, lock it into his memory, pull it out to savor in special moments for the rest of his life. The cold was no more than a momentary annoyance. The heat from Rory had begun to burn into his marrow.

From the instant the larger-than-life Scot had pulled him out of the crushing snowbank, his mouth filled with the taste of death, Alex had known he craved Rory Drummond. It was more than sexual need. And it wasn't an emotion born of gratitude. After his rescue, a huge sense of pure fucking gladness began to invade every waking thought, the joy of being close to that incredible man. At night, it seemed each dream began and ended with Rory Drummond.

It had to be love.

It wasn't like a choir of angels had descended, singing the hallelujah chorus. It was slow, hour by hour, a building of nerves and laughter and fear whenever they were together, until sometimes he couldn't even talk. Rory never pushed him, never asked him how he was feeling. And he, afraid to hear something he couldn't handle, didn't ask Rory. It was as though two grown men were one inch apart, yet afraid to move the fraction that would cement them forever or set them apart.

The reckoning was close. He had to talk with Rory now, or turn away forever. He could not, would not, walk away from this man. But how the fuck could he tell the Scot he'd been set on his tail like a fucking stalker, one hunter following another? How in hell would he tell the truth to the man he loved, when the feeling had been born from a lie?

They'd taken three days to hike almost three-fourths of the way up Moriah, and now the descent was too fast to assimilate. Right now, bumping and rattling down the almost-road from camp to the ranch, Rory at the jeep door and Alex's thigh riding his massive left leg, they did not speak. Alex had dared to put one arm around his waist in a way the driver would never see, and every so often he pressed slightly, letting his lover know he was not being aloof. Whatever he had to say would wait until the privacy of their cabin.

He'd been practicing his confrontation with Rory for days now, until he finally abandoned the whole scenario in disgust. *Just the unvarnished truth. Standing face to face on the harsh floor of the cabin, splintered and real. Just the truth.*

Their driver Tommy broke the silence. "You done good, fellas. Every man got a buck. Some got two. Now that's pretty unusual."

Alex smiled at him. "This trip has been great in every way. Something to talk about for years to come, right?"

"Steve will throw one hell of a farewell party, I know that. Don't fill your hollow leg, fellas. Hold that whisky for tomorrow night."

*Tomorrow night.*

Hell, by tomorrow night he'd be packing for a trip back to Elko, and Rory would be stowing his stuff for a plane ride to Edinburgh.

His lover must have been thinking along identical lines. They looked at each other in the same moment, and Alex saw his expression seemed troubled. *He must have something to tell me, too. How the crap are we supposed to say goodbye? Be sure to write... Call me sometime...*

Tommy pulled up as close as he could to their cabin and left the engine running while they unloaded the gear they'd thrown in the small back seat. They walked shoulder to shoulder, eyes locked, feet sure on the rough path. The small wooden structure hid the bed where tonight they'd spend maybe their last night together. The last tine they'd make love until ... until maybe hell froze over.

As soon as Alex unlocked the door, Rory took him into his arms. They began to kiss as though they hadn't eaten each other's face off already this morning as soon as they woke. Rory was the first to step back, apart yet still connected, running a large thumb along his bottom lip, tracing a line across the stubble of his chin to the hollow of his throat.

"Let me check my phone, lad, in case my father or Alan has left a message. I'll be back in a few minutes. Turn on the heater, warm the bed. I'm ready for the love making of a lifetime."

Alex remembered both their cells were being charged in Steve's office. He himself didn't care whether he ever reached civilization again. He'd check some other time. Of course, he didn't have a castle steward or a father five thousand miles away, like Rory did. A business to run. A family to worry about him.

"Make the world go away, Rory." He was echoing the words of a very old song, older than his own father, and he knew it. But his lover might think he was being poetic. Hell, he'd felt like singing a love song to the man as soon as the door had closed behind them minutes ago. But it could wait.

"I will lad. Just give me five minutes."

"When you get back, Rory, there's something I need to tell you. Something important."

Rory embraced him and kissed the soft skin just under his ear lobe. "And I have something to say too. I feel like a foogin adolescent. Get undressed and wait for me."

Alex nodded against his cornsilk hair and let him go.

After flipping on the space heater, he sat on the edge of the bed, head bowed, working his lower lip and his inner cheek, one after the other, then together, until he tasted blood in his mouth.

His own cowardice had brought him to this cliff edge. His fear of losing his job. His fear of another man actually loving him. His outright terror that as soon as Rory knew about him, he'd get on the plane back for Scotland; or at least demand that Alex take his lying ass back to Governor Suarez, tell him to fuck off, never talk to him again.

*This is it. What if he really loves me and wants to tell me? Before he can say anything, I need to tell him the truth. Let him save face. If he hates me for it, if he leaves me in disgust, at least I'll know I was finally honest.*

His heart was threatening to burst from his chest, and he felt a rising in his throat, a bitterness he couldn't swallow. When the door opened, he found he couldn't even raise his eyes to welcome the man he knew he loved more than his own life. The man who would no doubt change his world, no matter what happened next.

Head down, he sat forward with his forearms on his knees, and simply spoke to the splintered floor.

"Rory... Love... I haven't told you the truth. And God, I'm sorry. But I'm telling you now."

He needed to meet Rory's eyes, and he raised his head. The face he looked into was that of a stranger. A very tall man with red hair and a beard. But a face twisted in pain. Green eyes vacant, as though he was looking through him and past him. Not Rory Drummond, but a stranger.

He had waited a heartbeat too long to speak his heart, and now the heart was stilled. For ever fucking after.

\*\*\*\*

Rory Drummond was a man of the old school when it came to certain matters. He considered himself a drinker *par excellence*, one who both imbibed and appreciated many a fine vintage and every whisky to be found in Scotland, England and the continent. He saw himself as a lover of men, one who knew how to bring any partner to ecstatic climax, in several odd and amazing ways. His other virtues were legend: martial artist, scholar, horseman, outdoors enthusiast.

Yet nothing he had ever accomplished mattered a whit to him at this juncture of his life. He felt he was on the cusp of something rare, a new existence. One he would share with another, an equal partner.

All the way to the ranch, he thought about how he was going to confess the truth to his lover. *And the truth shall change your life, Rory lad.*

The truth was so simple as to be almost a cliché: He was in love. Foogin brogues over bollocks in love. He wanted to take Alex with him, keep him close for the rest of his life.

His intended was a man of principle, one who would be loath to give up his vocation for a whimsical confession of love. Hell, he'd already mentioned that his job was something safe and sure, a haven in his lonely life. Surely he'd never turn from a calling he'd spent all those years building, toward the time he could climb the next tier as a lawman. And why would he leave his heartland, the very soil he walked as a boy, to breathe the air of a foreign country? It was a stretch, and he knew it.

Rory also considered the fact that Alex was a man of restraint, almost to the point of being an introvert. No matter how impassioned Rory might be, he suspected his lover would not—could not—respond in kind. He'd have to murmur words of love to his shy Alejo and hope to see them reflected in the man's deep onyx eyes.

The descent from Mt. Moriah was happening too quickly. They seemed to be careening toward the ranch in the bloody lurching Jeep, where before they had taken small, sure steps. The past few hours had flown like a red deer on the Highlands, like birds soaring on autumn's final draft of warm air. Every image he conjured up was one of wildlife running, running, refusing to stop even for a moment, until there was nothing ahead but the final reckoning.

*Will you come with me, lad? Will you accept my love and stay at my side?*

Why in bloody hell hadn't he said something earlier? He had, actually, but in ways so subtle he'd surprised himself a few times. Like confessing he'd never made love to any man before Alex. Like giving the man his family crest. An object so precious to him he wondered even now whether Alex had the slightest clue what it might mean to a man who traced his lineage back almost a thousand years.

More than a few times, he thought he saw his own feelings reflected back in his lover's face and in his quiet actions ... a smile, a touch, a way of bringing his own impassioned body to the crest of joy.

After leaving Alex in the ramshackle cabin, he hurried to the ranch house, knowing Steve had arrived some time earlier to set up the arrangements for tomorrow. His host seemed to read his mind when he opened the door.

"Ah, Rory. Are you as wired into your cell as I am? Go ahead, use my office. Grab your phone, catch up on your messages. I'll be around here somewhere if you need me."

He followed Steve inside. "I am not so wired, lad. But my steward is. Alan Cameron. The one I let run my life so I don't have to."

Steve laughed. "Yes, my own guy Jack Warden comes to mind. Down the hall, first door on the right."

He opened the door to Steve's small jumbled office, appreciating the wrinkled old chair, sitting in it while he studied his phone. Several messages, all short, all reassurances of business going well. Good. Life was going to be simple, at least on the home front. He read the final message, and then he read it again. The words cut like a garrotte, stopping his breath.

*Robt. has set watchdog. Dominguez, lawman. Bodyguard & possible informant. Intel straight from G.L. Gang warily.*

He sank back into the infinite pouches and creases of Steve's leather chair, not caring that the cell phone had slipped from his hands and lay somewhere on the floor. His brain refused to make the connection between that handful of words and a man who was waiting for him a few minutes away.

*Dominguez. Informant. Hired by my uncle. Not foogin possible.*

*Intel straight from G.L.* That was Greer Logan, a woman of redoubtable talents. One who had been first a university classmate, and then a friend, long before she became the lover of Robert Drummond, man of Parliament and rising political luminary. She had always held their friendship above any amorous dalliances, and her word was gold.

His mind stopped working except for the dull beat that pounded *no no no no no* in time with his clamoring heart. Rory had no awareness of crying until Steve walked in and he raised his head from his hands, the palms slick with tears.

"My God, man. What's happened?"

Steve was squatting near his feet, his face crumpled and scrunched in concern.

"I ... have to leave. Right away." He said the only thing that mattered right now. He had to run, before the open gash could spill his heart and guts for the world to see.

Steve stood and hit the speed-dial on his cell. "Jack. Will you call the airport. Reserve the first flight that will connect with—" He held his hand over the receiver and mutely asked.

Rory heard a voice, maybe his own, a mere croak. "Dundee, Scotland. By way of Edinburgh."

Steve repeated that to his head wrangler. "Yes, of course. Yeah, one ticket. Let me know as soon as you can, okay?" He snapped the phone closed and put it in his back pocket.

"Just stay right here, Rory. We'll take care of everything. Can you tell me what's happened?"

Rory shook his head, absolutely determined not to mention Alex. The man's treachery was between the two of them, and no one else. "A very personal matter, Steve. One that takes me home. I am more sorry than I can express."

Steve set his hand on his shoulder and squeezed, a gesture of compassion. "Shall I have Alex bring your bags around?"

"No!" He stood up, frantic. The last person he wanted to see was Alex. But he had to retrieve his luggage. He would send no man to be his servant. "I ... I will do it myself. Thanks for your kindness."

Rory didn't know how his shaking legs carried him to the wooded copse where the little cabin stood, nor how he managed to open the door without crumpling on the doorsill. He saw Alex, still dressed, sitting on the edge of the bed with his head down, studying the cracks in the floorboards.

He looked up, and their eyes meshed. Rory saw his former lover's dark eyes smeared with a glaze of sorrow, his entire face a study in smothered pain. His lips were moving, but he heard a few words only.

*Love... Sorry...*

He turned and began to stuff clothing into his luggage. *No time to change clothes now. Just get the bloody hell out of here so I don't have to look at that face. Nothing he can say will change the past.*

He heard Alex talking but could not make out the words through the blood pounding in his ears. *Do not listen. Do not look. Do not prolong the pain.* He was sure anything he heard ... or the sight of a cherished face ... would make the memories all the more impossible to bear, and so he literally stumbled out the door without closing it and did not look back.

## Chapter Seventeen
### Getting outta Dodge

Alex closed the door and returned to the bed. He sat on one edge, feet on the floor, hands in his lap, and stared at nothing at all. The light came and went through the thin frilly bedspread hung on the window. The room slowly darkened until, looking down, he could no longer see even his knuckles twisting in his palms, could feel only the dull pain of his fingers digging into his own flesh.

He should get up, turn on the Coleman. Switch on the heat. But some kind of inertia had stolen the strength from his legs, had stripped him of the will to do more than lie back and stare into the dark, play with random thoughts that amounted to bullshit.

*Lie in a black shroud and think of nothing at all, and sleep will come... Swallow the crap that's filling your throat so you can breathe. You can do it, Alejo, Just like always before. No problemo. Shut it all out. Then get up early, pack, and leave. Don't think about the coulda and the shoulda.*

At first it sounded like his own ragged heartbeat. And then it got louder. A knock on the door.

*Rory...*

He sat up and shook his head to clear it. A strange voice sounded in the dark. "Come in." A voice he didn't recognize, a kind of guttural rasp that had to be his own. *Come in. Oh, God, Rory come in, come back...*

"Alex? It's Steve. Are you decent?"

The disappointment was as sharp as a sudden blow to his gut. He tried to clear his throat, tried to get up, couldn't find the strength to do either one. He heard his uninvited visitor entering, moving around, but he paid little attention.

He lost track of the time it took Steve to light the lantern and turn on the space heater. His visitor grabbed the one old wooden chair that wasn't heaped with socks and other crap, pulled it a foot from the edge of the bed, and sat. Leaning forward, Steve stared at him with those cold-chisel eyes for what seemed a full minute.

"I brought you a plate of food. It's out on the doorsill getting cold."

"Um, thanks ... I ... think I'm not hungry. But thanks."

Steve was silent again for a while. "I leave people alone, Alex. Let them fight their own fights, cry their own tears. Not because I don't care. Maybe it's ... hell, maybe I care too much sometimes."

He hitched the chair even closer. "Your father was a strong man. I know he taught you to be the same. So I won't say too much. Just know, Alex, a year ago I was exactly where you are right now. Fucking numb with grief. A loss I couldn't even comprehend. No one had died, but I thought I'd never see hi—see that person again. For a week I lived on a few bottles of stashed Christmas brandy. Forgot why God invented sleep, and what a tub was for."

Alex knew. That person must have been Cade Wilder. The sheriff, Steve's close friend. He'd seen the way they clasped hands the first day he'd met them, a subtle touch exactly like he and Rory had shared more than once when they thought others might be watching.

"I think I get it, Steve. You survived. You thrived, both of you."

He nodded. "Just want to say something you probably don't see. He loves you so fucking much he can't think straight. And neither can you."

For the first time in hours, Alex began to breathe.

"Someone, a friend, talked to me back then. Kind of like we're talking now. Not advice. Just helped me see I needed to start living my life a lot different. He gave me a job to do, like I'm gonna give you."

Alex felt a weak grin lift the side of his mouth.

"A job?"

"Yep. Nevada cops are a dime-a-doz. But I know you could start a new life, a new job somewhere else. Say ... even in another country."

He stood and put the chair back against the wall, opened the door, and brought in a platter of venison roast with a baked potato and a wedge of frozen butter, a knife and a fork stuck on top. "Eat this. I'll call Cade, have him stop by here in the morning and pick you up. He'll see you get to Elko. From there, you're on your own. Get it?"

Alex stood and held out his hand. Steve took it, a strong and warm grasp that spoke as loud as his intelligent eyes.

"When you get there, and I don't mean Elko, call me. Okay?"

When the door closed behind him, Alex sat on the edge of the bed again, thinking about what Steve had said. It was worth a try. He figured it would take him a while. But he could make a plan. He could turn his back on a decade spent in despair. Maybe he could do things differently, because he was a different man now. Because of Rory Drummond.

The drive north was uneventful, yet Alex thought it might have been one of the most productive trips he'd ever made. Because during that two-hour drive he met Alejandro Dominguez head-on, fought him to the bitter end, and won the battle.

Sheriff Wilder had arranged one of his deputies to haul him up to Elko under the guise of official business. It took a couple hours of pretending sleep in the sheriff's car for Alex to wrestle with his own conscience, deciding exactly what he needed to do five minutes ago.

*He loves you so fucking much he can't think straight.*

Steve's brief words had made a profound impact. The mere fact Rory was in love with him was a nugget he kept taking out and polishing, turning it every direction, finding in it whatever he needed to cope with his present loss.

He'd not slept at all last night, pacing and thinking, trying to come to grips with the fact he may never see Rory again. Steve had given him a job ... the job of pulling up the roots that held him to a dead-end present and going after the unknowable future.

Coward that he was, he'd held back from going to the ranch house for breakfast. No way was he ready to see his former lover's face, ravaged with whatever disappointment he might be showing.

Steve had finally stuck his head in the door around eight that next morning, told him Rory was gone, and for Crissake to shag his ass into grabbing a bite to eat, packing and getting to Elko. And here he was.

Letting the familiar highway be his emotional center, he began to relax inside somewhere, starting in his belly and working into his chest. For the first time, even counting the days he'd been with his lover, Alex thought he saw a flicker of hope. He'd turned his back on any kind of emotional attachment for almost a dozen years. Fear. Always the fear of rejection, punishment, ridicule. Fear of losing his job, then scared shitless Rory would leave if he told him the truth. Always fear.

And now, hope.

*He loves me. Steve saw it, when I was too dumb-ass to recognize it for what it was. Not just horniness, not just a bump in the night.*

*The truth is, I want and need and love Rory Drummond. If he boots my ass out of his castle, at least I'll know this time I gave it my best shot. No more sticking my head under a rock, hiding from myself.*

*Fuck my job. Fuck the governor's shitty assignment. And ... and fuck Rory Drummond. If he turns me away, I'll ... I'll foogin spank his ass until he sees the truth.*

Fifty miles out of Elko, Nevada, he turned his head away from the driver and cracked a brief grin before closing his eyes and giving himself up to exhaustion.

As soon as he shut the door to his tiny apartment in Elko and threw his bag on the floor, Alex pulled out his laptop and took care of the first order of business: getting his ass out of Dodge. Passport application ... done! Freaking nuisance, dealing with the State Department and the passport-issue people with their various hands out. But mission accomplished. It would be mailed to his current address within ten days.

He sat at the utility table in his kitchenette and mentally shuffled through the tasks he had to complete before he could leave. Type up report to governor's office... Type up statement for DPS supervisor... Get documents printed out... Shut down bank accounts and get travelers checks... Take passport photos... Make a plane reservation out of Carson City... Sell what he could and leave the rest of the crap behind. Buy some decent civilian duds... Put in notice to the landlord... Shut down utilities. *Yada yada yada.*

Ten days after he'd left the Long Trails Ranch, Alex firmly closed his apartment door, locked it, and slid the key under the manager's door on the way out. Then he piled into his old Dodge Challenger and hit the familiar highway west to Carson City, Nevada and the first man he needed to confront before facing Rory. That was Governor Escamillo Suarez.

\*\*\*\*

Real sleep was out of the question. Rory Drummond had gone many a night and many a week even, getting by on whisky and drunken oblivion. Just a way of life for a man whose feet never could find a straight path to home.

He remembered gesturing to Steve with the bottle. "Home, hearth and happiness. Right, lad?"

Steve had simply pointed him to a spare bed, when really the man should have put him in a foogin paddock with the livestock. He was that shit-faced, not worth two pence even to his mother.

He'd somehow undressed, then collapsed on the guest bed with a bottle of Johnny Walker Red, the whisky of choice for his host. It tasted a little flat at first, redolent of some of the cheaper blends he'd rejected over the years. But by God, just then 'twas all his heart's delight.

Even in the tongue-coated and head-splitting state of utter debauchery, he thought about Alex. His Alejo. Handsome, shy, reluctant Alejo.

*How the hell can that man be a spy? Or is he the world's best actor? And what the bloody hell was he paid to spy on?*

Lying on his back naked as a mother's babe, legs splayed like a defeated warrior, he pounded one fist into the yielding bed. Pissed that he'd hit only a bloody quilt, he rolled off the bed onto the floor and drove his fist into the wooden planks.

*How blind was I? Why couldn't I see the man was out to trap me?*

He was unclear about the entrapment. His uncle already knew he was gay. What would it profit him, having his own secret agent bed the man he was spying on? None of it made any sense at all.

The night went by in a blur. Someone or other came into the room and picked him off the floor, helped him dress, and then led him to the breakfast table, where he sat with his precious bottle. He barely remembered being strong-armed into the large van, and then finally sleeping on the way to the tiny airport. He knew he'd been damn lucky Jack had found a flight to Houston. At Yelland Field, someone, one of Steve's men, pushed a handful of tickets and baggage claims into his fist and poured him onto the plane.

On the way to Houston, Rory refused to let his shaking fingers compose an email to Alan. After asking the flight attendant to interpret his fistful of papers, he presented her with a green bill for fifty US dollars and asked her to enter the information: airline, date and time of arrival, gate number. He thumbed the button that would send the jumble of data to him and then asked for a very tall whisky.

He alternately woke, shuffled onto another airplane, drank and passed out again. At some level deep in his sodden brain he knew he was a barren waste. A man of erudite knowledge, impeccable taste, vast humor and studied insouciance. A bloody loser. A man brought low by the one emotion he'd managed to avoid his entire life.

*Love. Bloody sodding love. Aye, lad. Once smitten, forever doomed.*

The happiest moment of his trip home was collapsing finally in the arms of a worried-faced man he held dearer than most, his faithful steward Alan Cameron, who took him to Rory's own Mercedes and told him to stretch out in the rear seat. He vaguely remembered Alan and his father carrying him up the wide spiral staircase to his bedroom.

Drunk as he still was, Rory held on to one thought as someone stripped the Levi's off his ass and dumped him onto his bed.

*Robert Drummond, you bastard. Your turn is coming. As soon as I can foogin walk again.*

## Chapter Eighteen
### A Matter of Honor

This time cooling his heels outside the private office of Governor Escamillo Suarez, Alex was dressed in Levi's instead of trooper blue. He paid scant attention to the stiff leather under his ass, or to the overwrought furnishings. This morning, he was a man on a mission. He'd even brought a thin attaché case, something he'd bought so he could stash the ever-mounding pile of paperwork he needed to leave the country.

In his stiff new jeans and a nice dark corduroy western-style shirt, carrying a businesslike brief case, he felt almost sexy for the first time since Rory had left. But he refused to let his mind play with possible scenarios of them greeting one another. That is, if they got together again. *Whatever happens, let it just happen.*

An hour passed, and he began to get annoyed. It was ten now. His plane would leave at five. True, he hadn't made an appointment. But he'd stopped by George Braxton's office and talked for a moment with the secretary, the one who'd briefed him several days ago after his interview with Suarez. Braxton had assured him he'd put in a word, make sure the governor saw him for a few minutes. But no promise of when.

On the verge of walking back down the corridor to speak again with Braxton, he saw a lady in a dark business suit walk toward him and make eye contact. Her smile seemed to carry a secret message, a teasing he automatically ignored out of long habit.

"Mr. Dominguez. You have five minutes. I am sorry... The governor is between meetings right now."

He nodded with a polite smile, grabbed his case, and followed her undulating bum through the familiar heavy oak door.

Suarez looked up from a pile of papers on his immense desk. He flashed a smile, and Alex saw the glint of a gold back molar. For no reason at all, that sight curdled his gut and stiffened his resolve not to be a toady this time around.

The lady left, closing the door behind herself.

"I expected you to be on my list of appointments."

*Unspoken disapproval. Tough shit, Governor.*

"Yes. I've had to make a lot of arrangements in a very short time, drive here over some snowed-in stretches of highway. Unsure of when I could be here." No apologies, just the truth.

"Well, my boy, sit down. Present your report." He glanced at his Rolex. "I'm afraid I have a meeting in a few minutes..."

He did not sit. "Governor, my report will take thirty seconds to read." He placed his attaché case on the chair, opened it, and drew out two sheets of paper. In one step he reached the governor's desk and laid the papers in front of him, then stepped back a respectful distance.

Suarez picked up the top sheet and read aloud. His ironic tone suggested he was reading a political speech, complete with exaggerated flourishes of one hand.

"To the honorable E. Suarez, Governor of the State of Nevada: Pursuant to my assignment to escort a certain Scottish tourist in my job as Nevada State Trooper, I can tell you this with complete truth. I found the gentleman, Rory Drummond, to be without a doubt one of the most honorable men I have ever had the privilege to know. Every man on the hunt left with a profound respect and liking for him.

"In addition, Mr. Drummond proved himself to be such an outstanding hunter, trekker and outdoorsman he could have been the teacher and protector rather than myself. Certainly, he was in the same class as our experienced big game guide. Virtually alone, he saved one of the hunters from a dangerous snow slide.

"I count myself fortunate, and privileged, to have met him.

"Blah, blah, Alan Dominguez..."

He lowered the paper and glanced back up at Alex.

"So. Easy assignment. Excellent, my boy."

"No, sir."

Suarez frowned a little "No ... meaning what?"

"Not easy. And not excellent." He wanted to add, *And not your boy.* "I feel like my hands are dirty. I feel ... less than a man. If you will glance at that second report, please?"

This time Suarez almost mumbled, with no attempt to put dramatic emphasis on Alex's straightforward words.

"To the Governor of Nevada: Being the head of the Department of Public Safety of this state, you are the most appropriate person to receive this resignation from my job as Nevada State Trooper. Effective immediately. Alex Dominguez."

He tossed the paper aside and didn't pretend to smile. "I could have read this as I, ah, visited the toilet a while ago. Any reason you need to be here?"

"Yes, sir. I am a man of my word. I promised to complete the assignment. I said I'd present my report. I also want you to know my opinion, not stated on the report or in my resignation."

"Do I want to hear your slanted opinion?"

"Slanted? What—"

Suarez reached for the papers on his desk and brought out what looked like a newspaper clipping. "The Missoula Fair Press. Dated a week ago. 'Scottish visitor saves Nevada State Trooper.' Photo of a dazed man with snow in his hair, another photo of a large scowling man. One is you. One, I take it, is your savior. The man who pulled you, mighty trooper, from a snowdrift."

"May ... may I see that?"

Suarez pushed the clipping toward him, and Alex picked it up. The article had been written by Drew Farley, no doubt a reporter for the Montana newspaper. The one who'd spent time quizzing him about his job. The one who couldn't seem to keep his digital camera in his pocket or his eager smile from Rory's face. It all made sense to him now. The real spy, the real tracker out for a sensational story, was one he never would have suspected.

He glanced at the article, designed to make him look like a fool. A trooper who fell in a pile of snow and had to be pulled out by some tourist. But this was the first time he'd seen Rory's face since he'd walked away, his patented way of half-scowling with one lip tucked into his mustache. The sight of it made his heart itch. He desperately wanted that picture.

"May I keep this?"

"My secretary always files duplicates. You have my permission to ask him. That one shall remain with your report."

He stood. "Now if you will excuse me..."

"Governor, this article is stupid. Written to deceive, to sell newspapers. I really *was* buried in an avalanche. The man came to my rescue with no thought of his own safety—"

"Nevertheless. His 'brave actions' had to skew your opinion, young man. If he was a drunk and a total idiot, you'd have reason to defend him. It makes little difference to me. But it makes me not unhappy to accept your resignation. You have burned your bridges. I doubt you'll ever work in law enforcement in this state."

*Never forget, Alex, this is a political animal, not quite a real person.* "One last matter, Governor Suarez. I need to tell you why I'm resigning."

Again Suarez glanced at his watch.

From somewhere inside, Alex managed to call on his buried talents as a data presenter, back in some forgotten college forensics class. "I think a Nevada State Trooper was placed in a position of being a liar and a fake. Yes, Governor. In spite of his stated wishes not to accept the assignment. I think ... I'm sure one call from Washington, some political favor or mutual washing of hands, placed a state employee in a potentially dangerous position. Certainly in a position to be seen as a coward and a fraud."

"That's ridiculous."

"Just my opinion... Sir. And I won't be afraid to repeat it. To the press boys here in Carson City, to newspapers in Washington, D.C. and to the Scottish Parliament as a body. That's how strong my feelings are."

He took a deep breath. "A dozen men on that trip will give the lie to your newspaper article, and then how will that make you look? 'Nevada Governor plays political payback games with his law enforcement men.' Or maybe, 'Suarez spends thousands of tax payer dollars in ice-capades caper.' Now I'm afraid I have no time to chat with you, sir. I have work to do."

He turned and walked to the door.

"Alex."

The governor was already standing behind him. Alex was amazed the little man could move so fast, especially from the immensity of his marble desk. He turned around slowly to face him, saying nothing.

"I'm sorry we've had a small understanding. Even though you agreed to the assignment, it was rather a ... shall we say, unnecessary one. And so is your resignation."

"No, my mind is made up about that, Governor."

"Well, if you ever want to move up, perhaps to another position in law enforcement here in Nevada, or in some other State capacity..."

"I just want my story told fairly. I want my report given to the one in Scotland who asked for it. Just as I turned it in. No crap—excuse me—no hint that my report is biased in any way. Because it is not."

Suarez stood a moment, his unusual brown-black eyes thoughtful. "I agree to do that. I give you my word. Is that fair enough?"

"Will the newspaper story be left here?"

"Yes."

"Then yes."

He opened the door and left before the governor could stick out his hand in some sort of "we have a deal, wink-wink" gesture. Because the only deal was, Suarez would be honest. Alex himself had agreed to nothing at all.

He stopped by the secretary's office and got a duplicate of the newspaper clipping, which he held until he left the building. Once outside, he sat in a small portico shielded from the early November wind and smoothed it on his knee. He didn't care to read the story, just a mesh of half-truths. But looking at Rory's dear face, his hands began to shake just a little. He opened the case and put the cut-out newspaper in a leather flap, then closed the attaché.

His plane for Los Angeles was leaving this afternoon for New York, then on to Scotland. In hours—not days—he would see Rory Drummond, or else fucking drown in the Atlantic trying.

\*\*\*\*

Rory cautiously opened one eye. It was morning. Again. He knew, behind the heavy draperies, the sun was trying to fight its way past a typical late October cloud bank. Or was it November already? Another gray day, another bottle of whisky. No sense trying to eat breakfast. Especially since he knew his father would be glowering at the table, ready to pin his bollocks to the sideboard with a butter knife.

He winced. Avoiding his father had been almost as difficult this past fortnight as avoiding thoughts of Alex. Both men were poised to fell him. One with baleful eyes under shaggy red brows, the other with brooding black ones watching him from the veils of memory. He'd been using any excuse to stay in his room just so he wouldn't have to talk to anyone about ... him. The one who had seized his horns and hide and left him ruined, a trophy for his wall.

Before he could do more than sit up, his bedroom door opened, then closed. He looked up to see old Kenneth Drummond five feet from the bed, dressed in a wrestler's work-out robe.

"Um,'tis a fair day, then, father? You are up early."

"No. I am very late. As you are. I've come to chat with you about business."

"And what business is that, sir?"

"If you don't know, lad, I foogin give up. Get out of bed. Dress if you must. But stand up and face me like a man."

Rory grinned and stood, not bothering to seek a pair of underwear. It was a damn lie that a Scot never wore underwear. If it was cold enough, he'd put on a pair of Aussie Bum undies. But only if there was a threat of hypothermia to his scrotum. Right now it was only natural to face his father like a man, as he'd been bidden.

Kenneth Drummond had been one of the best kick boxers of a generation. He shrugged off the robe, and Rory sourly noted two naked men standing within three feet of each other in the oversized bedroom. He also noticed that his father, even at the ripe age of fifty-two, had not seemed to lose even an inch of well-toned muscle. *When does this man work out? And why? I need to spend a little more time at home, I see that.*

Rory tried to grin, but it was wiped off his face by a foot so swift he hadn't seen it coming, one that landed just behind his ear and caused him to stagger back a few feet.

"Again, lad?"

Before Rory could answer, his father whirled and sent a kick to his solar plexus. This time he ended up sprawled on his ass on the Oriental carpet.

"Foogin pathetic. You have two choices. Take care of business. Or I take back lairdship of Drummond Castle."

Rory tried to get up, failed, then looked up at his father with a grimace. "What do you mean by 'business,' Father?"

"You know, lad. I mean this. And this." He thumped his chest in the region Rory suspected meant his heart, then his head. "You will foogin come 'round to the facts of life, or I'll have to admit I have no son. Only a little girl hiding under the bed."

In a flash of intuition, Rory understood his father had been busy during his son's many absences. He was a force to be reckoned with. And he was bloody tired of cleaning up after his spoiled progeny.

He extended his hand, and Rory grasped it, heaving to his feet. He stood with his arms crossed, staring at his father.

"I admit it. I was—put on my ass. The same way you just did. By a bloody pair of dark eyes. He betrayed me. I left. It will take time, Father. But I will rejoin the human race."

"Starting in exactly twenty-four hours, lad. You have been, ah, summoned to my brother's place of business. Begin there."

Rory shook his head as if to clear a cloud settling over his cerebral cortex. "You mean his Scottish Parliament office?"

"Just so. I have a feeling there is something between the two of you needs settling. I will keep the home fires burning. You take care of Robert. Then shag your ass back here and take care of those very fires."

Kenneth Drummond never ceased to amaze him. Just when he thought his father might be slipping at last into his peaceful years of warming by the hearth, he bloody well seized him by the balls and showed him his mettle.

His father extended his hand, and Rory grasped it, and then his forearm. "I love you, old man."

"Save it, lad. I already know. Tell it to the man who needs to hear it."

He turned and left the bedroom while Rory contemplated how in sodding hell his father had known. And how best to deal with a meddling uncle.

Almost as though the past two weeks hadn't happened at all ... as though it were scant seconds from the time they'd last sat in this room together... Robert strode indolently to the liquor cabinet and raised the decanter, one brow arched in a mute question which Rory gladly answered.

"No whisky today, Robbie lad. Ah, make it water."

Robert quirked one eyebrow and brought him a glass. Not a goblet, not a shot glass. A foogin water tumbler. As though it was a peace offering.

Both men settled back. Rory had worn his dress kilt again, in deference to the marvelous site of Scotland's Parliament. He thought his own splendid dress would be a tribute to Miralles, the Spanish architect who'd so clearly seen into the soul of an entire nation of Scots. This time he did not flash his thighs in an attempt to embarrass his clansman. Today called for even cruder tactics.

His uncle wore a morning jacket of satin with a brocade vest, thousand-dollar trousers, black brogues, and a carefully crafted smile.

"So. Tell me about your trip, nephew."

Rory had already decided the cat-and-mouse games were over. "You tell me, Robert. What exactly did Dominguez report to you?"

Robert almost lost his composure. He covered his surprise by taking a sip of whisky and regarding him over the rim of his own goblet.

"I'm ... afraid I don't follow you."

"The spy. The one whose nose you stuck up my asshole. The one you paid to mark my every move. *That* Dominguez."

For once, Robert seemed nonplussed. "Honestly, lad, I don't follow. Apparently you somehow found out I was, ah, concerned for your well-being. I may have asked a colleague to speak to someone who spoke with the Governor of that immense state you visited. A gesture of family concern, no more."

"You must know the name."

"Yes, I do. It came to me not long ago on a report. A glowing report, I might add. I've had it downloaded from the governor's email."

He stood, walked to his desk, and brought a thin file to the sofa where Rory sat. He fingered a piece of paper as if considering whether to share it, then handed it to him.

*...without a doubt one of the most honorable men I have ever had the privilege to know... I count myself fortunate to have met him.*

What he'd just read was as forceful a blow to his solar plexus as the one his father had surprised him with yesterday. He felt the air leave his chest, found himself speechless for once, staring at words swimming on a typed page.

He finally found his voice. "I don't bloody understand. You hired this man to spy on me. And now you show me his espionage work."

"Hired him? My dear nephew, I never bother with the little people. You know that. He was what Americans might call a willing dupe. Merely a policeman trying to follow orders." He grinned and tipped his glass again. "One lazy Mexican, the Governor, calling on another to do his duty."

His uncle's act of showing him the report had somewhat softened Rory's resolve to teach the man a lesson. Yet now his elitist attitude and blatant racism swung the pendulum back to all-out retribution.

Rory set the page on a side table and stood. He kept his voice low, controlled. "If what you say is true ... I am humbled by what this man had to say. It makes me want to really be such a man. God knows, honor and I have seldom walked hand in hand."

Robert nodded, a knowing smirk on his face. "So relax, lad. As they say in America, no harm, no foul. Eh?"

"Wrong!"

Rory stamped one foot, annoyed that it did not make a resounding boom on the thick carpet, and then he smacked one fist into his palm inches from his uncle's nose. *Smaccck!* Robert blinked.

"You have finally tipped the scale, Robert Drummond. The stalker may himself be stalked. How do you think I found out about your sneaking behind my back? How do I know where you went two nights ago in Edinburgh ... that small Swiss cabaret where no one knows another man's face?"

He'd made a calculated guess on that little revelation, based on a brief phone conversation yesterday with Robert's mistress Greer. She'd remarked that when he went to the city, be sure to visit the Swiss Chalet, a circumspect little cafe where he could drink and eat all he wanted. Where someone would tuck him into a discreet bed, with or without a mate, and all for a reasonable price. She herself had gone there the previous evening with a certain date. No names mentioned, of course.

He had opened a vein, he saw that right away. Robert's face had paled, and he would not look him in the eye.

"I will not be followed, ever again. Do you hear? You will respect me as your nephew, as a man, and as a human being. Or I promise, your election campaign may suffer a few embarrassing press conferences. Am I clear?"

Robert stood. "You are."

"Then my business here is done."

Robert actually looked stricken. "I apologize. Let this not stand as a wall between us. Please, Rory. My career, your life. Both shall remain separate from now on. I promise you on my mother's grave."

Rory grinned. "Your mother is the reason I do not call you a son of a bitch, lad. She's also my dearly departed grandmother. Good day."

They shook hands, and he left. Yet he knew it would be only a matter of weeks before they'd be playing hide-and-seek again with each other's affairs. Old habits die hard. This time he didn't care. He had a whole new lease on life.

The words in Alex's report coursed in his veins... *Could have been the teacher and protector rather than myself...* Alex had seen himself as a mentor and guardian, not a spy... Fortunate, and privileged, to have met him. Almost two weeks of whisky had numbed his brain to what must have happened, if only he'd had the balls to look squarely at the man Alex had proved himself to be. A good man, and true. One who thought of his job as a pledge of honor. One whose honest feelings showed unfailingly in his luminous eyes. A man who just possibly once loved him...

As soon as he found a moment of privacy, he'd place an emergency call to the police in a village somewhere in a sagebrush tundra. A place called Elko, Nevada.

# Chapter Nineteen
## The Refuge

From the Parliament Building in Edinburgh, Rory took a taxi to the airport and caught the hop to Dundee, a small city just thirty kilometers from home. He met Alan at the terminal with a smile that cracked his face for the first time in weeks.

"Home, my laddie. And keep the whisky away from me. I need to think straight."

He settled back on the passenger seat of his Mercedes sedan, his phone in hand. Alex had not betrayed him after all. Why the foog did he ever believe it? Because his sources were rarely wrong. Greer Logan had the correct information, no doubt tongued from the mouth of her lover Robert Drummond. But now, looking more clearly, he reckoned that's how all intel had the potential to be a lie. Correct man, wrong interpretation of facts. Stalker with cunning intent? Merely a lawman, asked or told to do a job.

He thought about Alex being used by his superiors, tried to put himself in the man's brogues. Tried to imagine his thoughts and feelings when they met ... when both of them seemed to fit the contours of each other from the moment their eyes locked. Alex must have been bowed with guilt from the beginning, even though he had done only the wrong of not telling him. And yet to his employer, keeping the mission from Rory was the crux of the assignment.

Rory let his mind dwell on the man's own drunken lapse that night of Steve's welcome gala, his anguished admission that he was a fraud. He sat staring at the phone in his hand as if it had morphed into his lover. He tried to imagine the burden Alex must have carried, along with the pent-up grief from his past, a burden he could never bring himself to fully confess.

He fingered the phone, wondering what he would tell Alex if he could get through to him. *I've drunk myself into a stupor, I've lost precious time. What do I tell you that will stop an avalanche you didn't start? How do I dig you out this time from the crush of my own folly? From the arrogance of the bloody assholes who set it all in motion?*

By the time Alan Cameron had driven him home, Rory was thoroughly depressed. After several attempts to call the U.S., he had finally reached the only law enforcement office the overseas operator could find in Elko, Nevada. The tinny voice which finally responded told him she was a dispatcher. Assured him that yes, this was the place where Nevada State Troopers were headquartered; but no, the man named Alexander Dominguez was not on the roster of troopers. No, apparently he had left some time ago. How long? Oh, maybe a week? The voice was not sure. Could someone else help him? What is this call about?

*'Tis about two men who've lost each other, madam. And may never find each other again in this lifetime.*

Getting slowly out of the car and walking into Drummond Castle, Rory had already lost the surge of hope which had briefly lifted his shoulders. Before he could walk up the sweeping stairs, hoping to evade his father, the man appeared out of nowhere. He seemed to block his way subtly, a mute command of attention.

"Business completed, lad?"

"Aye, Father. Or maybe, in a way, just begun. I'm home this time to think instead of drink."

Instead of tucking his mouth into his typical ironic *moue*, his father rewarded him with one of his rare jubilant smiles "Then by God, I'm ready to step aside as vice-laird. Your new affairs begin now, Rory my son. Ah, my lovely wife calls. Your darling mother has summoned me. Don't expect to see me for supper."

He winked and walked from the large foyer, leaving Rory a little bemused.

*Father is ready to cede castle affairs to me? I've been away so bloody often, what makes him think I'm ready to handle it? And why this sudden emphasis on "my son," "your darling mother"? Father is more an enigma the longer I know him. Reminding me my first priority is family, is he now?*

He reached the second landing and looked down on the chandeliered foyer, the grand entrance to the only home he'd ever known. A little bigger than what he'd admitted to Steve Long, and one which called for more than an absentee landlord ... the kind of man he'd become. He'd turned his back on family, driven by his need to find whatever he'd been chasing.

Before he walked into his bedroom, Rory let his hand rest on the door lever, arrested by a sudden insight. *I think I've been chasing Alex, without knowing it. He was always there, and I've been trying like bloody hell to find him. And as soon as I found him, I walked away from him.*

When he entered, head down, already beginning to remove the pin from his woolen kilt, he walked from force of habit to his favorite chair. Old and worn to the shape of his own buttocks, the overstuffed relic had remained in his room in spite of all attempts by his household staff to burn it. The only piece of furniture in the castle he thought of as his own. He remembered Steve and his own wrinkled piece of crap of a chair. *Some things you need to let a man keep forever. High on the list is a place to sit that doesn't chap his bollocks. The other thing? Most important? That would be the man he loves.*

When he raised his head, he saw the interloper. The only man on the face of this earth he'd ever allow in his place of refuge. Rory had to shake his head and squeeze his eyes shut for a moment, sure his mind was still affected by the gallons of whisky he'd sluiced through his brain and his gut this past fortnight.

*Bloody foogin hell. Am I dreaming?*

\*\*\*\*

Any other time in his life, Alex knew he'd be either numb with indecision or shitfaced from drink, hiding from his fears. Funny how a fleeting few days in a man's lifetime could retrain his brain to see himself and the world differently. Since the moment he'd walked out of Suarez's office, Alex felt he'd become a man of iron purpose. Here he was, walking the same soil as Rory must have walked a thousand times. So close he could almost see the man's eyes, feel them penetrate his fucking soul.

He knew precisely what he had to do.

He'd gotten off the plane in Edinburgh, asked until he found an answer. Castle Drummond? *You need to be in Dundee, lad. Not so far.* So he'd switched to a plane for Dundee. There he'd summoned a taxi, found a driver who'd take him to the castle. It turned out there were at least three such castles, but only one close to the ocean. He remembered Rory spoke of having a sailboat. Yes, there was a Clan Drummond domicile in Arbroath, county of Perth. Not so long a distance that an enterprising fellow could not take an American tourist. For a price.

The trip to his former lover's home was a blur as he spent the time staring at his hands and wondering how in the world he could penetrate a castle keep, find a way to reunite with Rory. He was conscious of stopping outside an immense gate of a smallish, quaint, and very old castle. He remembered paying the driver in strange currency, then asking him to stay until he came back to retrieve his luggage—or to take his leave, by order of the castle laird.

The memory of being escorted into a chandeliered drawing room was just a fleeting impression of understated wealth. But every faculty of his brain snapped into sharp focus the instant he saw the man who stood waiting for him under the tiers of sparkling lights.

He was almost Rory. Very similar to his lover, with streaks of silver in the russet hair and twenty years added to the expression on his face. Alex saw where the look had come from—that half-scowl, a lip strangely configured into the mustache.

The handsome man wore a kilt, the tartan predominantly red with muted plaid in blues and greens. The shirt was white, long-sleeved with an open collar, and the gleaming black wingtip shoes were no doubt the very latest in highlander brogues. Alex felt a flush of embarrassment, seeing how this Scot was so damn masculine in what he once thought of as a "dainty skirt."

The huge Drummond extended his hand. "Kenneth Drummond. Vice-laird of this castle. Rory is expected back sometime today."

He returned the man's very firm grasp. "Alex Rodriguez, sir. A friend of your son."

"My son has, ah, many friends, Mr. Rodriguez." Alex saw the man subtly size him up, maybe deciding he was another of Rory's minions. "May I ask how you know him? Forgive me, but being temporarily in charge today, I must serve as the dragon at the door."

Looking squarely into the man's ocean-green eyes, he removed the gold chain he'd been wearing around his neck the last few weeks, the one on which he'd strung a certain heavy gold crest. Silently, he handed it to his host.

Kenneth Drummond stood for maybe thirty seconds staring at the ornament on the pendant before handing it back to him.

"Do you love my boy, Alex?"

"Yes, sir. I do."

"Then you and I have something important in common. Welcome to our family."

---

Someone saw to his luggage. A slender silver-haired man, no doubt a valet, escorted him up a wide spiral staircase, and from there into a vast room dominated by a king-sized bed. A Rory-sized bed.

It was fitted with a canopy, large as a freaking circus pavilion, whose flowing draperies revealed silk pillows on a silk spread. A bed fit for a king, a castle laird, a man who needed space both to sleep in and to fuck in. Alex felt his cock begin to get curious.

At the foot, below a set of stout dowels, sat his two bags, all the possessions he owned from a lifetime of not accumulating worldly goods. He had rued giving up his old muscle car, trading his title for a handshake at the Carson City airport, but the regret had lasted all of ten minutes.

The man awarded him a tiny uptick of his mouth and a kind expression in his eyes. "The laird's own chambers. Please enjoy your stay. You may summon assistance ... there." He followed the man's eyes to a velvet cord hanging near the dowels of the immense headboard.

The valet inclined his head slightly and left Alex to prepare himself for the second most important meeting he'd ever experienced. The most critical one was the day he'd turned around in a tiny airport and met a man larger than life. And now he'd somehow have to meet that same man and convince him he'd never lie again.

He removed his boots and padded across several thick Oriental rugs to the bathroom, a space almost as large as the apartment he'd lived in. In the center, raised on curved porcelain legs, sat a tub that reminded him of a swimming pool. It was free-standing, the faucets and other mysterious bronze appliances—a douche maybe—anchored to a vast marble-tiled floor. This room obviously was part of a curved turret or some kind of dormer because the ceiling sloped toward one end, and the far wall was hexagonal with a wide window that let light enter through a pale yellow, silky drape.

Irrationally, he thought of a simple yellow chenille bedspread drawn across the window of a rustic cabin. His cock twitched again.

Next to the vast tub was a Victorian-looking chair of red velvet whose back and legs were festooned with bronze-gold metalwork. It sat next to an impossibly fancy dressing table with a tawny yellow marble top that echoed the silken drapes.

Rory had told him he spent most of his time away from the castle. Looking around the oversized room, from the large potted fern to the gilt frames of expensive paintings on the walls, Alex could not blame him. A man who craved the dirt under his boots and the cold blast of mountain air might feel a little too damned civilized in this place. In a bathroom that looked like a freaking ballroom with indoor pool.

Fingering the precious pendant like a good luck charm, he took a wiz into an ornate toilet and left the room. He thought briefly about stripping, taking a bath, losing the stink of untold hours on several airplanes. *No sense getting too comfortable. Rory may tell me to hit the road, and I need to be ready.* He knew that was the old Alex speaking. But it made a lot of sense. He had no earthly way of reckoning whether his former lover would believe him now, after knowing him only as a man who'd deceived him.

He sat in a comfortable chair close to the bed, letting his rump settle into the soft recesses. *I'll just rest my eyes for a minute ...* he thought lazily of an old tale, something about Goldilocks and a very large, very sexy bear.

He gave in to his exhaustion. When he woke, he sensed someone was standing close, watching him.

He saw the tartan first, the same colors as the one Kenneth Drummond had been wearing a while ago. Yet this kilt was much heavier, a wool blend, possibly meant to be worn in cold weather; and instead of being drawn shut with a large ornamental pin, this one was invitingly askew. Subtle and yet, like the man, disarmingly open.

*Rory.*

He'd awakened knowing he was sprawled in Rory's comfortable old chair, legs outstretched, his chin on his chest, and he found his gut clenching as he raised his eyes from the kilt to the face.

His former lover was standing a few feet from where he half-assed slouched in the chair, his hands on his hips, his head cocked. Alex saw the familiar expression of confusion mixed with scowling disbelief.

"Alex?"

He forgot to breathe while he struggled to sit straight in the chair and look into Rory's eyes, searching for a sign of acceptance.

"I ... am sorry ... ah, sorry if I'm bothering—"

*Fuck.* He thought he'd changed from the coward Rory knew all too well. But the sight of that rugged, handsome face and soul-searching, sea-deep eyes clawed at his chest. The man's frown, the furrowed disbelief on his face, made him sense a stark emptiness, a raw need where his heart used to be. He seemed powerless to move.

"Aye, lad. You bother me. Yet not in the way you seem to think." Rory knelt on one knee a foot from his chair and extended his hand, a tentative move, almost like he was reaching out to touch a shadow. Where the flap of the kilt had fallen aside Alex saw his full groin, the hanging sacs and immense erection, not at all hindered by his astonishing choice of clothing.

*I could grow to love a kilt. Very quickly.*

He managed to pull his eyes from Rory's crotch to his face. What he had to say had nothing at all to do with the man's generous endowments. "I wanted to tell you in person, Rory. What I tried to tell you that ... that last night at the ranch..."

Suddenly Rory smiled, an expression which filled his eyes with festive lanterns, like a celebration.

"Five thousand miles is a long way to come, lad. This must be important, what you need to say."

Rory's palm enclosed his cheek, and then his forefinger began to trace the line from his jaw to his mouth, as if memorizing it all over again.

Alex swallowed, hard. He hadn't dreamed it would be this difficult. But this time he looked directly into Rory's bottomless eyes. "I never meant to hurt you. But I was a fucking coward and never told you the truth. So I'm telling you now. When it may be too late."

By now Rory was cupping his face and looking so keenly into his eyes Alex thought the man must know what he had to say, but he somehow dredged up the guts to spill it anyway without flinching.

"I love you. Then and now and forever."

# Epilogue
## The Crest

As soon as Rory saw Alex Dominguez asleep in his favorite chair, he knew the truth. Yet he still stood a few feet from him, allowing his heart to rattle his ribcage, not trying to talk down the rampant hard-on that threatened to lift his heavy walking kilt. He waited for the lad to tell him the secret, the words he'd been half-crazed needing to hear, and wanting to speak out loud, these past few weeks ... the words which kept getting lost somewhere in the bottom of a whiskey bottle.

After a while came the moment of truth. The shimmer in Alex's dark eyes, the lift of his chin and mouth. *I love you. Then and now and always*.

He gathered the raven-eyed man to his chest and sought his mouth, murmuring and whispering as he bit and sucked. *Mi caro, Alejo mio*. The soft answering pull of Alex's teeth on his bottom lip, a mouth opening to accept his jabbing tongue, the frantic sucking and biting ... all of it soaked his brain and hit his deep gut like the whisky of the gods. More, more, he needed to take his man now and never let him go.

They were nested somehow in the folds of the big chair. "Let me take you to bed, *caro*. I need you..."

With a visible effort, Alex pulled back from his arms as though he were being suffocated. "Wait, wait, Rory. This is more than boy loves boy. We need to talk..."

Rory dipped his head to his lover's throat and nuzzled for a moment, breathing in the musky odor he craved. He worked his way back to the beloved mouth and spoke in between kisses.

"We will, lad... Ah, God, Alex, we will talk... I promise..."

Alex brushed his beard with his fingers, stroking, entangling, letting go. He smiled. "You haven't asked me why I'm here. What I'm—where I intend to stay. How long I'll be here. Our ... special relationship. All of that is important to both of us."

"Then tell me, lad. I'm listening."

"Okay." He saw Alex take a deep breath, as though his next words might be as hard to say as his first. "First of all, I've ended up here with two bags and myself. So I don't have a clue what the hell I'm going to do. I can't just rent out a space in your castle. I don't want to hurt your feelings. But I refuse to be your pampered lover."

"No, lad—"

"Wait."

Alex put a finger on his mouth as if to hush him, and he wanted to take it in, suck it, let it become the prelude to instant lovemaking. But Alex moved his finger away. "I need to find my bearings, get a job. I want to live in Scotland, if they'll allow me. I need us to understand what we intend to do. Both of us. As ... as a couple, and as individuals, too."

Rory pulled back so he could really look at Alex for the first time since he'd embraced him. The man's eyes were burning with the kind of deep emotion he'd craved in his dreams, both besotted and sober. He saw the important fact blazing from those remarkable eyes: Alex loved him.

But he saw also the strain around his mouth, the impatient shake of his head. And he started to listen closely to what he said. Obviously this man would never consent to moving into his bedroom, being his indolent lover, taking his time to putter around the castle. No, Alex in his way was much like Rory's own father. Independent, willful, proud.

"'Tis a coincidence you ask, Alex. My father and I were just discussing how I need to, ah, control my wanderlust, and my whisky too. I need to be the man I say I am. A castle laird. A man of responsibility. And now with you at my side, that new role will be all my joy. I promise you. We'll work it out. We'll spend time fashioning a real life together. Not boy loves boy, but man loves man. All right?"

Alex smiled, that pouty little droop of his lip which curled one side of his mouth into a dimple. "Who loves who?"

"Whom."

"Tell me."

"Quiet, lad."

He pulled Alex from the chair and laid him on the bed. It seemed not so different in that moment, in this place, from the first night they'd lain together in the motel room. Then and now ... Alex splayed in front of him fully dressed, his eyes gathering twilight, going darker with lust.

"I have ached for you, Alex, every day and night." He straddled his lover and began the chore of pulling buttons from their holes, an odious task made delightful by the smooth dusky skin he was revealing, the pink fruit of his ripe nipples. And lying like a crown between his breasts, a familiar token. His own crest. His ardent confession of love.

His heart leapt, nearly choking the air from his chest.

Alex fastened his deep-set eyes on him. "Then tell me."

"What, lad?"

"What you need to say. What I need to hear."

"We're not bonnie lasses, Alex. You already know."

"Tell me."

He seized the metal button of the Levi's, but it was a new pair and the hole was too small to yield to his fumbling fingers. He cursed and leaned close to Alex's belly to remove the offending trousers, but Alex slapped his hand away with a stinging whack of his palm.

"You are as much a coward as I cursed myself for being. Tell me, goddamn it, or I get up right now and leave."

He grinned, loving the game to come. "You have not the balls, lad. I will have you, with or without your foogin consent."

"You've almost taken off my shirt. A shirt for a shirt, you prick. Sit still."

Rory relented and loosened his legs' grip on his lover.

Alex rolled from beneath his pinioning thighs and knelt in front of him on the bed surface. He unbuttoned his dress white shirt with nimble fingers and slid it off his shoulders. Rory did the same with his lover's dark western shirt, not quite sure of his fingers, yet loving the feel of the heavy corduroy. Both of them flipped their prize onto the floor, and both of them reached for a nipple at the same time, pulling and squeezing.

"Let me suck, lad."

"No. My turn, damn you."

And then they were wrestling, trying to reach a nipple, laughing, nearly rolling off the bed.

"The kilt next. Kneel in front of me, Rory."

What had happened to the shy, reluctant man he'd left with head bowed in that little cabin? Instead of unbuckling the sides of the kilt, Alex ducked his head under the tartan, licking his balls while squeezing his butt cheeks.

"Ah, God, Alex—" He dug his hands into the man's shoulders, letting the ravening mouth grab and suck, slaver and move up his shaft.

Alex's moiré hair emerged from beneath the kilt, and he straightened again, still gripping his ass, while Rory threw his head back, his throat vibrating with moans of pleasure. Grasping fingers became smooth palms on his ass cheeks, massaging and coaxing, until his cock reared to its fullest, a champion stallion desperate to be given its head.

Alex fingered and stroked, smiling at him. He had no sensation of the kilt being unclasped; and yet somehow it lay in a muddle at his knees.

"Your turn, lad." He grasped the waistband of the Levi's and twisted the hateful metal button, managing to loosen the denim and pull at the zipper. "Come here." Rory hardly recognized his own voice, thick with passion. This taunting man had intentionally driven him to the point of shaking thighs and a prick that was already too full. The thick seed began to leak until he felt it along the length of his straining flesh, oiled and ready.

Alex embraced him, keeping him close, his tongue in the sensitive inner ear. "You are wrong, *hombre*. It's my turn. I need to know you'll trust me from this day on. Will you?"

Before he could speak, Rory felt a stinging slap to his ass that gripped the inside of his hole and seemed to escape from the slit of his cock.

"I will—try—to..."

"Goddamn it, I said you need to trust me."

Alex was strong enough to grasp his upper arm with one hand and send another painful *thwack* to his butt cheek. Rory leaned into his lover, needing to climax, tonguing his mouth. "Ah, Christ and all the foogin saints of heaven, I need you. I trust you."

But Alex had gripped the base of his prick, squeezing off the blood flow. He felt the cum trying to bubble from his balls, yet rudely ambushed by this man bent on punishment. Another slap, more exquisite pain.

"Yes, love, yes. I trust you."

"Then lie on your back with your knees up. And wait for me."

He lay on the broad expanse of bed, on the verge of erupting on the ceiling, while Alex climbed off and squatted at the end, near the foot dowels. When he came back, he was bare as a babe except for one thing. A pair of alligator skin cowboy boots. In spite of his crying need for release, Rory smiled, remembering.

"Now, Rory, you will tell me what I want to know. Raise your legs."

Rory could not take his eyes off Alex as he dove between his legs and began to lick the strip between his balls and his asshole. He began to arc his ass, then lower it, faster and faster, trying not to moan. Alex's fist again gripped the root of his cock, cutting off his need to fountain his cum everywhere. A slick tongue rolled around the rim of his asshole, a slavering and slobbering, convincing him he was about to die right on this bed and go straight to heaven or hell.

And then Alex straddled him, lifted his balls, and sank his broad cock straight into his hole. He felt the thick cowl rub the inside, then withdraw, until he was desperate to be filled and slammed to glory.

Like the athlete he was, Alex bent and began to kiss him, driving his tongue deep, all the while his cock was slicking in and almost out, in and nearly out again. "Tell me, goddamn it."

Rory tried to tell him the words, moaning the lyrics to a song of deep-seated need, and he felt his inner walls begin to spasm.

They both began to climax, the release a flood of ecstasy. "Alex, Alejo." He sobbed into his lover's mouth while the convulsing flesh found his innermost secret.

Afterwards, his lover lay on his chest, so close he heard the man's heart speak into his own. He raised his head a little and sought Alex's dark eyes, finally answering him.

"*Te quiero, Alejo*. From the moment I foogin saw you. I love you."

## THE END

# About The Author

**Erin O'Quinn** sprang from the high desert hills of Nevada, from a tiny town that no longer exists. She hopes her voice carries the simple, deeply resonating tones of men and women who live close to the earth and who find their spiritual center there.

Erin's published gay novels are the following, available widely:

**The Iron Warrior Series**
Warrior, Ride Hard
Warrior, Stand Tall

**The Noble Dimensions Series**
Noble, Nevada
The Chase
A Hard Place (short story)

**The Gaslight Mysteries**
Heart to Hart
Sparring with Shadows
To the Bone

**Wilderness Trails Series (with Nya Rawlyns)**
Bighorn
Night Hunters
Mustang


These are Erin's blogs devoted to gay themes:

The Man in Romance: http://romancemanlove.wordpress.com/
Ac´cent Gay Lit Authors: http://gaylitauthors.wordpress.com/
MM: Gaslight Mysteries: http://caitlinfire.wordpress.com
WILDERNESS MEN website (with Nya Rawlyns):
http://wilderness-men.weebly.com/index.html

NEVADA HIGHLANDER

Made in the USA
Charleston, SC
28 December 2013